Nobody's Baby

Nobody's Baby

Penny Kline

Published by Accent Press Ltd 2015

ISBN 9781783758203

1

One small high-pitched sound, like the ping of the phone that suddenly stops, leaving you in suspense. A wrong number, or had the caller changed his mind? At five in the morning the news could only be bad.

Later, much later, when the full horror of what had happened had sunk in, Izzy would look back on that moment and remember how sorry for herself she had felt. Tragedy puts your own problems into perspective, but that cold autumn day she had no inkling of what was to come.

She was sleeping alone. How can you be both glad and sorry someone is not there? Glad that the person who caused you so much pain is no longer around to inflict another wound. Sorry because your creation, the man you wanted him to be, has gone from your life, leaving an empty aching space.

Three weekends had passed since she told Josh to pack. At first he had refused to believe she was serious. When he realised she meant it his jokes had turned to anger. Piling his belongings into four cardboard boxes and a zip-up bag, she had refused to cover the same ground again: the arguments over bills and the lies, some of them so elaborate, so pointless, like those of a small boy who wants to get one over on his mother.

When challenged he had looked crestfallen, an expression he had perfected. Yes, she was right, his mother had been strict as hell, so pushy, so ambitious for him that he had never felt he could live up to her expectations. Now she, Izzy, was forcing him to face the same feelings all over again.

Except I'm not your mother, she thought.

Since his departure, weekends had been the toughest. Weekdays, work days, were more or less bearable. Kath and Harry to talk to, a drink at the pub, more drinks at home, then crashing out around eleven.

When the sound woke her, she had thought Josh was lying next to her. She missed the feel of him, the warmth of his hard, smooth back, and the smell of his hair. At least the house was hers. Two up, two down, with a tiny kitchen tacked on the back and a garden the agent had described as 'a useful barbecue area'. Thinking about it reminded her how she and Josh had brought Blanche home as an eight-week-old kitten, let her out through the back door, then watched her investigate every nook and cranny as if she had been released into a garden ten times the size. Who did Josh miss the most, her or Blanche – or were they both just ancient history?

Now wide awake, Izzy listened. The sound could have come from next door, through the thin dividing wall – except next door's house was for sale and the occupants had moved out five weeks ago. To her knowledge the estate agent had only shown a handful of potential buyers around, and the 'For Sale' notice was still firmly attached to the ground-floor window.

There it was again, another high-pitched cry, and this time she was sure it was in the street. Swinging her legs over Josh's side of the bed, Izzy crossed to the window and held back the curtain, waiting for her eyes to adjust to the darkness. Everything looked the same as usual – pedestrianized road, stone container with a single standard rose that should have been pruned a month ago. Orange light from the street lamp, twenty yards up in Palmerstone Road, picked up dappled raindrops on the parked car. No one was about. Everything was silent. The sound must have come from a cat, the black and white tom from opposite, out on the prowl searching for a mate. Not Blanche; she was safely asleep on the basket chair.

Returning to bed, Izzy lay on her stomach, wondering if Josh was sleeping alone. The living-room floor of Dave's poky flat was not the ideal place to take a new conquest, but knowing Josh he could well have ousted Dave from his king-size bed. *Come on mate, I'll owe you one.* Was there anyone Josh had ever come across who was not owed one?

The wail that interrupted her thoughts bore no resemblance to the night call of a cat. In an instant she was out of bed and running down the stairs, missing a step and almost falling headlong. The cold, damp weather had made the door stick and as she wrenched it open she stubbed her toe and cursed, then almost tripped over the dark shape in front of her.

The carrycot had been pushed up close, probably to make sure it was covered by the slight overhang of what had once been a porch, and the baby inside it had stopped crying and was lying very still.

Izzy crouched down and touched the pale forehead, then jumped as the eyes opened and the wailing began all over again. Lifting the cot, she carried it into the house and placed it on the sofa, clicking on a lamp then moving it when the light shone too fiercely on the tiny, blinking face. The room was cold – it was too early for the central heating to have come on – but the baby was wrapped tightly, swaddled, so that only the head was visible. Pulling back the blue blanket Izzy put her hands round the warm little body and lifted it out, holding it awkwardly against her shoulder, patting its back, pressing her cheek against its woollen hat.

For some reason it seemed important to establish if it was a girl or a boy. The hat was blue and white so that probably meant a boy. Dragging at the poppers on its yellow sleep suit, that were harder to free than she expected, she caught sight of a slip of paper next to a baby's bottle, half full of milk, and a disposable nappy that had been wedged between the blanket and the side of the cot.

The baby was making noises in its throat. Izzy laid it on top of the blanket, hoping that would not produce another bout of crying, and held the slip of paper under the light. It was written in block capitals and the ink had smudged a little, although the letters were still clear enough. HER NAME IS CRESSY, she read, TAKE CARE OF HER.

'Cressy.' Izzy removed the baby's hat and smoothed the tufts of hair, apologizing for the coldness of her hands on its skin. Not "it", a girl baby and so small she could only be a few weeks old, possibly only a few days.

A dribble of milk had dried into a crust at the corner of her mouth. Izzy touched it with a finger and the baby's head turned, searching for food. Stretching out to reach the bottle, she offered it to the open mouth but the baby jerked her head away and started to yell, her face quickly turning red, her eyes screwed up in frustration.

Perhaps the milk needed to be heated. With the baby balanced against her left shoulder, she hurried to the kitchen, found a pan, half-filled it with water, and switched on the ring. Outside, the engine of a car sprang to life and Izzy paused, listening. The sound came closer and she hurried back to the other room, peering through the window, thinking, irrationally, that it could be the mother who had changed her mind and was returning to reclaim her child.

The car had moved out of sight, but looking out into the street reminded her that her first response should have been to call the police. What was she doing, warming milk, jogging the baby on her shoulder, breathing in the smell of her skin and holding her up so she could see through the window? For a split second, she thought she smiled, but it was only an involuntary pursing of the lips. Babies were incapable of smiling until they were five or six weeks old and even then, according to the books, they responded just as enthusiastically to three blobs on a sheet of white card as they did to an actual face.

As she watched, the round blue eyes struggled to focus then relaxed into a squint.

'Cressy,' Izzy said again, speaking as you might to a stray dog with a disc on its collar. The baby smacked its lips, searching, and Izzy found herself moved to tears by the knowledge it had no idea what had happened to it, that its only aim was to find something its mouth could latch onto.

Not it, her. Holding her steady with one hand, Izzy lifted the phone with the other and rehearsed what she was going to say. My name is Izzy Lomas. A baby has been left outside my house. I think she's only three or four weeks old.

How bad would someone have to feel before they wrapped their baby in a blanket and left it on a stranger's doorstep? Surely these days, however desperate your situation, there was always social services – or a hospital. She had read about a teenage girl who left her baby in a hospital foyer. What happened to abandoned babies? Had anyone ever found a baby and decided to keep it, moving to a different area, pretending it was her own, that she had given birth at home, that the father was unknown, that she had not received any antenatal care?

'Police, fire, or ambulance?' asked a flat voice with a strong West Country accent, and Izzy returned to reality.

Harry was out of the office, but Kath greeted Izzy with the news that the psycho contract, as she called it, had to be completed by the end of the week so they would need to work flat out.

'Right.' Izzy's brain felt muzzy from lack of sleep.

'Hey, are you OK?' Kath pushed her thick mane of hair behind her ears, revealing large shiny hoops, and came up close to Izzy, examining her face. 'No, of course you're not. Time heals, but not that fast. If only there was some way we could speed things up, tablets you could take, I dunno.'

'If you invented one you'd make a fortune.' Izzy sat down at her computer and closed her eyes. 'Anyway, it's not Josh.'

'What's happened?'

'Outside my front door. A baby. Someone left it there in the middle of the night.'

'Oh no!' Kath's voice was high-pitched with emotion. 'Was it dead?'

'As far as I could tell it was fine, it was a little girl, only a few weeks old.'

'How could you tell? No, silly question. Oh, you poor thing. What kind of a person could do a thing like that?'

'I don't know.' Kath would want to know every detail, what the baby had looked like, how it was dressed, how big it was, what Izzy had done with it.

6

'She's been taken into care,' Izzy told her, 'the police are going to let me know when they find the mother.'

'*If* they find the mother. And why your house? I once heard about a child that was found in a wheelie bin at the back of the supermarket. You called the police, did you, then what happened?'

'They got in touch with social services and a social worker came and took her away.'

Kath pushed back her chair, almost knocking it over, and crossed to Izzy's desk to give her a hug. 'Oh, Izzy, you sound so sad. Is it because of the baby or because of Josh?'

'I'm all right. Just a bit tired. I imagine the mother chose my house because of the overhanging piece of roof where Josh never finished taking down the broken porch.'

'Could be I that, I suppose.' Kath looked doubtful. She was wearing a scoop neck leopard-skin top over a lime-green T-shirt, and it made her skin look sallow. An American, brought up in Ohio, she was a few years older than Izzy, and very different than her, but in spite of this they had hit it off at once. Maybe they complemented one another: one quiet, self-contained, the other noisy, outgoing, with a tendency to cry at the drop of a hat.

Izzy's thoughts returned to the slip of paper pushed down the side of the carrycot. The scrawled message. HER NAME IS CRESSY. TAKE CARE OF HER. Somewhere, a long time ago, almost as though it was a dream, she had come across that name before. In a book was it, a film? Cressy. Cressida. Her befuddled brain struggled to remember, but it was no good.

Kath was peeling the foil off a new jar of coffee. 'You don't imagine it has anything to do with Josh, do you?'

'Josh? No, of course not, how could it?'

Kath shrugged. 'Just seems a bit of a coincidence. He

7

was bound to take it badly, you giving him his marching orders.'

'Marching orders' was hardly the way Izzy would describe it. For the third time in as many weeks, he had returned home in the early hours of the morning. What was all the fuss about? He and Dave had gone to a club with a man who might put up some cash so they could start their own business. Yes, he knew he should have phoned, but when he noticed the time he was afraid she might be asleep, and in any case his battery was flat.

'Sorry,' Kath said, 'that was a stupid choice of words. You know me, smart on the spatial side of the brain, hopeless at anything verbal.'

It was an in-joke. They were working on a graphics package for a company that marketed psychological tests. Test your personality: take an aptitude test and stop feeling like a square peg in a round hole, choose the right partner for a fulfilling relationship.

In spite of her interrupted night, or maybe because of it, Izzy had reached the office early and found Harry literally running round in circles, searching for a file and complaining he was going to be late and his car was parked on a double yellow line.

There was something different about him and it took Izzy a moment to realise what it was. His hair. Instead of falling across his forehead, it had been cut short on top but left sufficiently long at the back that it still curled round the lobes of his ears. It accentuated his slightly debauched look, something Izzy found mildly attractive, perhaps because it reminded her of her father. He was wearing a suit but with a sweater instead of his usual collar and tie, and if Izzy had not known him better she would have suspected some woman had been trying to give him a more up-to-the-minute look. Not his wife, Janet, who appeared to have as little interest in Harry's appearance as she did in her own. Perhaps it was Harry himself, aware that he was approaching his fiftieth birthday and in need of a new image.

He was on his way to Bristol, he said, too busy to look at her or he might have noticed something was up, had to meet a client to discuss a possible contract to produce the brochures for a string of health clubs. The whole thing had been arranged in a rush but he would be back by five at the latest to check how they were getting on.

'Yes, all right.' Izzy had felt upset, as though Harry had deliberately decided to be away from the office just when she needed to talk. Kath was a good listener, the sympathetic one, but telling Harry would have put the whole incident into perspective whereas Kath liked to wallow in sentimentality. Who was it who said sentimentality is only sentiment that rubs you up the wrong way, and why did she feel so tearful? The baby had trusted her – it had no choice, poor thing – and she had handed it over to the police, wrapped up warm in its carrycot, together with its bottle and the spare nappy. Should she have changed its nappy? There was no time. The police had arrived in a flash.

'I need to get a grip on myself.'

'What?' Kath asked, and Izzy realised that, without meaning to, she had spoken the words out loud.

'Nothing. I was just thinking.' A baby. It was just a baby. She needed to distance herself from what had happened. It was gone, swept up into the system. She had no claim to it. She was simply the person outside whose house it had been abandoned.

'You say the poor kid had its name pinned to it?' Kath had left a bright smear of lipstick on her mug and was rubbing at it with a tissue.

'No, there was a note, pushed between the blanket and the side of her carrycot.' *Cressy, her name is Cressy.*

'You didn't recognise the handwriting?'

'It was block capitals.'

'Well-formed or those of a more uneducated person?'

It was a ridiculous question. Better not to talk about it any more. 'I've no idea, Kath, I expect it was written in a hurry. I imagine the mother was in a pretty bad state.'

'Cressy's short for Cressida, right? Don't think I've come across anyone with that name – apart from the one who had a thing about Troilus. What about you?'

Izzy had started work but something about Kath's voice made her turn round. 'What are you thinking? You don't honestly believe there's something I haven't told you, some reason my house was singled out specially?'

'Did I say that? No, of course not. Forget it, you're right, time to put the finishing touches to the publicity material. Harry wouldn't see having a kid left on your doorstep as any kind of an excuse for falling behind with your work.'

Shortly after six o'clock a detective knocked on Izzy's door. The bell was broken. Josh had insisted it was his job to carry out small repairs and she had gone along with his allocation of tasks, even though she could have fixed it herself and Josh never did today what he could put off until tomorrow.

The woman, who announced herself as Detective Sergeant Linda Fairbrother, had golden skin, large rather beautiful eyes, and a mass of curly dark hair held back by a blue band. She had not been on duty when Izzy put through the call, she explained, but had been assigned to try to trace the baby's mother.

Izzy stared at her. 'You're a detective? It never

occurred to me the CID would be involved.'

'The media's our best bet.' She accepted Izzy's offer of the most comfortable chair. 'So far we've drawn a blank but it's early days yet. The press have been informed that the baby was found by a woman living in this area, but don't worry, no name or address so you won't have your privacy invaded. Not that there's much you could tell them, is there?'

'Where is the baby?'

'Foster home in Dawlish.' DS Fairbrother was gazing round the room as if she thought it could have some bearing on the case. 'Nice people, she'll be well cared for.'

'Can I see her?'

'You want to see the baby?' Fairbrother thought about this for a moment. 'I don't see why not. I expect it could be arranged. Couple with two older kids, both fostered. Plenty of experience.'

'What will happen if you can't trace the mother?'

'We will. You get the occasional abandoned child that remains unidentified but …' Her voice trailed away as she stood up, crossed the room, and stared out at the small back yard. 'Have you lived here long? On your own, are you?'

'Until a few weeks ago I was sharing with a friend.' Earlier on, Izzy had lit a candle and the scent of mixed spices – it was supposed to be soothing – filled the room.

Fairbrother had her back turned. 'Pleasant part of the city.' She picked up the portfolio case that Izzy used when she needed to bring a design home with her. 'You're an artist, am I right?'

'I work for a small graphic design company.'

She nodded. 'You've no idea who could have left it here?'

'The baby? Of course not.' Izzy had prepared herself for the question but it still threw her. 'Whoever it was probably thought the bit of overhanging roof would keep the rain off.'

'Possibly. It was a cold night. I imagine whoever left it assumed it would be found fairly quickly. No one knocked on the door or rang the bell?'

'No, I explained when I phoned. Because the street's been pedestrianized it's relatively safe.'

'So you haven't a clue who the mother might be, or the father come to that?'

'If I had I'd have told the policemen who came round last night – I mean this morning.'

Fairbrother ignored this. 'If it did belong to someone you know, or someone who knows about you, knows where you live, it would be a compliment of a sort.'

'How do you mean? Oh, you think ... No one I know has given birth to a baby during the last few ...' Izzy broke off, frowning, checking in her mind that what she was saying was correct. A friend of Josh's? With a dull thud in the pit of her stomach, it even occurred to her that Josh might be the father. 'How old is she? Presumably she's been given a thorough check-up.'

'Four or five weeks. The carrycot's second-hand but there's no harm in that. People spend ridiculous amounts on their kids these days. Right, I think that's all – for now. If you want to see the baby I'll have to square it with social services and the foster parents.'

'It's just ... It was such a shock, finding her like that.'

'Sure, I understand.' Fairbrother gave her a cold smile. 'I'll be in touch.'

As she started towards the front door, Izzy switched on the passage light and they stood for a moment facing each other.

'So.' Fairbrother's face gave nothing away. 'If you think of anything that could be of help, give us a call. By the way, this friend of yours who moved out, what's his or her name?'

'Josh Lester.'

'And where is he living now?'

Izzy gave her Dave's address and watched as she wrote it in her notebook. 'It's only temporary, for all I know he may have moved on.'

'And his job?'

'Technical manager for an IT company. Look, he doesn't even know a baby was left outside my house. If he'd heard he'd have been in touch.'

Fairbrother opened the front door. 'Chances are you're right about the porch. Some poor kid got herself pregnant. Bloke did a runner. After she had the baby she struggled on for a week or two, trying to make a go of things, then found it too much.'

Izzy watched her walk away towards Palmerstone Road then turn her head, probably to check if Izzy had gone back into the house.

'Something else you remembered?' she called.

Izzy shook her head. 'Sorry I couldn't be more help. Let me know when I can visit the baby. I just want to make sure she's all right.'

It was well after midnight but Izzy's thoughts were racing and she knew from bitter experience if she went to bed she would lie awake for hours. Why did she have a feeling there was something important she had forgotten to do? Something at work?

After Fairbrother left she had phoned Kath but only heard the familiar message. Where was she? She had said nothing about going out for the evening but then why would she? Once they had spent almost as much time together away from work as they did at the office. Then Josh had come along.

For a time Kath had been keen on a bloke called Justin, but it hadn't worked out and Izzy had felt she was letting her down, spending so much time with Josh. Not that Kath had complained. She was not the resentful type.

Disappointed that Kath was out, she even considered calling Josh's number. Because it was hard to stop thinking of him as the most important person in her life? Because if the baby had been left on her doorstep a few weeks ago, Josh would have been there too and it might have changed things between them? But why would it? If she contacted him he would take it she was having second thoughts, missed him, wanted him back. He would be round at the house in minutes and the pleading would begin all over again. Or would it?

At his twenty-fourth birthday party he had told her, in an alcohol-induced state, that he was tired of playing the field, wanted something real, needed to commit. And she had believed him. Because she wanted to, because she was in love with him. Remember the day we met, he had murmured, pulling her hard against him. Remember when I came into your office to install the new system? I remember, she had told him, waiting for him to describe all over again how he had known immediately that she was the one.

The sofa still had a slight indentation where she had placed the carrycot. Closing her eyes, she tried to recall the tiny features, the pale hair and soft, slightly blotchy skin, but it was not the memory of the baby's face that caused a sudden intake of breath.

Cressy. In an instant she was back in Chester, sitting on the floor in her friend Dawn's bedroom, playing their

14

game, with Dawn's mother Rosalie calling to them, asking what was so secret they had to keep the door closed.

Rosalie Dear. It was a strange name. The name of Dawn's father who had died when she was still a baby. The game. What was it you had to do? Touch the other person's fingers one by one and chant a special rhyme. "If you had a baby and it was a girl what would you call it?" Then you bent back the finger you had reached and refused to let go until the other person had thought of a name.

She could picture it so clearly. Dawn sitting cross-legged with her grey school skirt pulled over her knees and her long Sasha doll hair covering most of her face. She was self-conscious about her breasts that had started to develop when she was nine although they never grew very large. And Izzy, who would have given anything for Dawn's blonde hair instead of her own indeterminate brown, had never been very sympathetic.

In her mind's eye, Dawn was laughing, jabbing at her fingers. 'If you had a baby and it was a boy what would you call it?'

'Elliot. Ow! Don't, I said Elliot, I'd call him Elliot. Come on, Dawn, it's my turn now.'

They must have been ten, the year they had to choose a secondary school although it went without saying they would both go to the comprehensive that was already attended by Izzy's brothers. Later they would both gain good grades in their exams, although Dawn's were always that little bit better and Izzy had had to work that little bit harder. After they left school, Izzy had gone to the local art college to do a one-year foundation course and Dawn had left Chester to go to King's College, London, where she was to study Maths and Philosophy.

'If you had a baby …' Izzy could hear herself reciting

the words in the mechanical drone they had perfected. 'If you had a baby and it was a girl what would you call it?'

And Dawn, pulling her hand free and flinging out her arms. 'Cressida! I'd call her Cressida. I would, Izzy, I really, really would.'

There was only one thing for it: she had to find Dawn. And the only hope of finding Dawn was to talk to her mother.

2

Was the time difference between England and New Zealand exactly twelve hours or did it depend which island you were phoning? Izzy decided it was safe to call and, as usual, was surprised when her sister-in-law picked up the phone, sounding as if she was speaking from just down the road instead of several thousand miles away.

'Laura? It's Izzy.' She listened to the warm, friendly greeting then asked if it was possible to speak to her mother.'

'Of course. She's out the back with the kids.' Izzy listened as Laura called her mother's name then disappeared into what was probably a large garden, or did they call it a yard?

After her father died, back in February, her mother had sold the house in Chester and moved to West Somerset. Neither Izzy nor her brothers had thought it a good idea, but if it didn't work out she could always move back north. However, during the six months she had spent in the village between Minehead and Porlock she seemed to have settled in well. Then Izzy's brother Dan had written, suggesting she spend a couple of months in Christchurch. Izzy had expected her mother to turn down the invitation, or at least put it off until the following year, but she had jumped at a chance to see her grandchildren.

A loud familiar voice came on the line asking, a little anxiously, if everything was all right.

'Yes, fine, I just thought I'd give you a ring, see how you were enjoying yourself.' She was talking too fast. Her mother would guess something was up but she would not press her. She was always so tactful, so diplomatic, and as a child Izzy had longed for her to lose control, shout, swear – especially at their father.

'Nina and Kirsty have grown so much,' her mother was saying, 'you'd never believe it, and Nina's got beautiful golden hair like Dan's. You must come out when you have your next holiday. Dan and Laura would love to see you.'

'I might do that.' Izzy cleared her throat, as though to alert her that she was going to reveal the real purpose of the call. 'One of the reasons I phoned, the night before last ... something rather strange ... a baby was left on my doorstep.'

'What kind of a baby?'

'A little girl about five weeks old. She's been taken into care, the police have no idea who left her there. .'

'Was she all right?' Her mother's tone was wary, the way she always sounded if she thought the conversation might be moving towards something upsetting. Like the day before Izzy's birthday when her cat had been found behind some bushes, dead. Izzy had sobbed, refusing to accept that Pushkin had gone to heaven, but her mother had insisted he was having a lovely time, playing with all the other cats that had died, and in a week or two they would look for a new kitten. Just what Pushkin would have wanted!

'Are you still there, Izzy?'

'Yes, sorry. Yes, the baby seemed to be fine. Actually there was one other thing. Rosalie Dear, have you heard from her ... ' She was going to say 'since Dad died' but was unable to say the words. 'Do you know if she's still at the same address?'

'Rosalie?' Her mother gave a tense little laugh. 'It's odd you should ask. I had a letter from her after your father died but I've heard nothing since, even though she used to be rather a good correspondent. And for some reason she's not on the phone. And of course she'd never have a mobile one.'

'But the last time you heard she was still living in the house she moved to when she left Chester?'

'Yes.' She paused and Izzy wished she could see her face which was always such a giveaway. 'Tell me about your job. And Josh, how is he?'

'Josh's fine. I may be going up north soon, just for a few days, on business. Only I thought if I had the time I might call in on Rosalie.'

'Good idea. She'd like that.' One of the grandchildren was urging Granny Sylvia to come back. 'Just a moment, darling. Sorry Izzy, Kirsty's tugging my skirt. Hang on, you wanted Rosalie's address.'

'No it's all right, if it's the same as before it's in my address book. Oh, just one more thing, when you heard from her did she mention Dawn?'

'Dawn?' Her mother broke off to whisper something to the child standing next to her. 'No, not a word. As a matter of fact, I was thinking you ought to check with Dawn before you go and see Rosalie, just to make sure she's not away on holiday or something. Anyway, it's lovely to hear from you. I feel rather bad, being here for Christmas. Still, you and Josh are probably quite relieved I won't be expecting you to visit.'

'Don't be silly. The thing is, I'm a bit worried about her.'

'About Rosalie?'

'No, Dawn. I haven't heard from her for ages. She wrote, saying she and Miles were coming back to England, but since then nothing.'

There was a short pause at the other end of the line. 'How strange. The two of you were always such good friends. We were all relieved when she left that religious place and joined you in Devon, but what a waste to throw in her Ph.D. – for a Portuguese man too, and didn't you say he was married?'

'Married, yes. Portuguese, no.'

Her mother gave a short laugh. 'Anyway, when you see Rosalie, tell her I'll be in touch quite soon. I'll ring off now or you'll have the most fearful phone bill. Bye then, Izzy, I'll write and tell you all the other news. Oh, and love to Josh.'

The journey should take about five hours, longer if she stopped off in Chester. Her initial intention had been to travel there and back in a day, but the weather was bad – intermittent rain with brief spells of wintry sunshine – and the travel news had warned of a hold up near Birmingham.

Did she really want to visit her father's grave? The memory of his sudden death was still raw. And there was something else, something that was making her uneasy, depressed. Threats to her self-esteem were usually the root of the trouble, a stray remark taken personally when it was not what had been intended. Something Rosalie had written on a card, sent to her mother a year ago. *Such a shame about Izzy and Dawn – they used to such good friends.* Used to be?

Driving up the motorway in her insulated bubble was soothing for a time. Then it became monotonous. She decided to pull into services and as soon as she did she had her first real sensation of travelling north. Ordering coffee, she looked up at the menu of hot food. Perhaps she should eat a proper lunch so she could dispense with an evening meal.

Her thoughts were interrupted by a large round-faced woman behind the counter, who was busy extracting slices of bacon from their bath of grease.

'Something to eat, pet?' The woman's hair was pushed into a green and white cap and beads of sweat stood out on her forehead. Along with the rest of staff, she had probably been up since dawn, waiting to be picked up in a coach and transported to the restaurant – from Wolverhampton or Bilston. Did she enjoy the work or was she just glad to have a job?

'Looks good,' Izzy told her, turning away from the smell of frying and trying unsuccessfully to lift a cheese bap with the plastic tongs provided. 'But I'm not very hungry.'

'Here you are, pet.' The woman slid the bap onto a plate with her hand then turned away to talk to her colleague behind the counter.

Moving towards the checkout, Izzy had to wait while a smartly dressed woman searched in her handbag then gave up, frowning impatiently at the bald-headed man who was helping himself to soup of the day. Motorway services were strange places. Neutral ground. No man's land. The woman with the handbag reminded Izzy of her mother, and memories of Chester that she had been suppressing since her father's death came flooding back. Playing in the garden. Her mother hiding, jumping out on them with hysterical shrieks. Laughing. Always laughing.

During the rest of her time on the motorway, she listened to the CD of *Barchester Towers* that Kath had given her the previous Christmas, losing herself in the intrigues of the clergy and only returning to the present when she passed junction fourteen and realised the next exit led to Nantwich, then the A51 to Chester where she had now decided to stay on the ring road and avoid the city centre.

When she reached Nantwich, the sun came out. So much for the weather becoming worse as you travelled north. For an hour or more she drove past farms and garden centres, through villages that followed the route of the Shropshire Union canal, until she reached the outskirts of Chester. Traffic was heavier than she had expected and in no time she was lost, circling the city centre, catching glimpses of the cathedral and the river, before finally spotting the road to Hoylake.

By the time she arrived at her destination, the sky was overcast again and, as she approached the estuary, the wind battered the side of the car. According to Dawn, the water had once lapped against the stone wall at high tide, then the river had been artificially forced to slow down along the opposite shore. Now it remained far out beyond the grass-covered mudflats. Grass-covered, but you could still smell the mud and it was extraordinary how a smell could bring back such vivid memories.

Once, years ago, she had gone there with Dawn and been shown the house where Dawn had lived until she was eight. Her father Graham had worked in Liverpool, travelling each day to Birkenhead then through the Mersey Tunnel. When he died – Dawn had still been a baby at the time – she and her mother had stayed on, then Rosalie had decided their life was too restricted, that it would be better for Dawn to live in a city.

Part of Izzy wished she had invited Kath to accompany her – Kath would have enjoyed a weekend in Cheshire – but another part of her needed to travel alone. If she had explained about the name Cressy, Kath would have insisted she tell the police – and she would have been right. As it was, Izzy was giving herself a few days, a week at the outside, to find Dawn, then if that proved impossible she would confess her suspicions to DS Fairbrother.

Where *was* Dawn? When she arrived in Devon eighteen months ago, they had been pleased to see each other, and Izzy had been delighted Dawn had given up the religious cult that had kept her a virtual recluse for the past three years. But they had grown apart, the differences between them magnified by time. Izzy had struggled to recreate their friendship, talking about shared experiences from the past, but Dawn had been strangely reluctant to join in. The past was the past, she seemed to be saying, they had changed, moved on.

Landmarks looked smaller than she remembered, distances shorter. When she turned the corner and saw the mudflats stretching out towards the river, her heart began to beat faster. Just as she had known it would, the scene resurrected an old recurrent nightmare. *Slimy mud threatening to suck you under. A desperate struggle to decide on the least dangerous option. Was it better to move slowly, carefully, testing each step, or to run wildly for the shore, praying your feet never touched the ground long enough for you to be sucked in?*

Tufty grass covered the hard mud close to the sea wall. The place was rather attractive, not threatening at all, and staying the night there could be quite pleasant. And seeing Rosalie? When she found her – if she found her – would Rosalie be pleased to see her or would she greet her with a cold, uncomprehending stare? *Izzy? Where have you sprung from? I'm afraid I'm rather busy ...*

As a child, Izzy had never given much thought to the fact that Dawn had no father. Since he had died when she was still a baby, Dawn herself had no memory of him and only knew his name had been Graham and he had worked for a large clothing company in Liverpool. Once, Dawn had shown her a photograph of him, standing leaning against some railings, a shortish man with sandy hair and sucked-in cheeks, quite nice-looking in a way, quite romantic, but perhaps that was only because he was dead.

Standing a short distance from Rosalie's house, Izzy tried to work out what kind of reception she was likely to get. How had Rosalie felt when Dawn announced she was giving up her research degree so soon after arriving in Exeter, and going to Portugal to live with another woman's husband? If Rosalie had been angry, upset, then Izzy might be the last person she wanted to see. Of course, if Rosalie knew about the baby ... But how could she? The most Izzy could hope for was that Rosalie would provide information that made it impossible that Cressy could be Dawn's baby. In that case, she could return to Devon with a clear conscience.

Somewhere in the distance, a single church bell tolled. Rosalie could be attending family communion. In the past she had never been a churchgoer but people changed, turned to religion for comfort and support.

Between two narrow strips of multi-coloured gravel, a concrete path led up to a bright blue front door. Something straggly and prickly had been wound in and out of the wrought iron fencing and some of its red berries had fallen onto the pavement and been squashed under the feet of passers-by. Two front gardens up, an old man was busy scraping the contents of a pan onto a bird table. Wooden spoon in hand he stared at Izzy, registering an alien face with a small degree of interest then shuffling back into his house and slamming the door.

The way Izzy remembered her, Rosalie had never liked anything flashy, preferring to spend what spare cash she had on books for Dawn, so the blue front door with its shiny brass fittings was a surprise. The flat in Chester had always been clean and tidy, but in contrast to Izzy's home it had been very simply furnished, with curtains Rosalie had made herself and pictures and ornaments picked up from stalls in the market. For a time, she had worked for a mail order company that 'paid a pittance' but allowed her to do flexible hours that could be reduced during the school holidays, although from the age of eleven Dawn had been left on her own for whole days. Both Dawn and Rosalie had appeared perfectly happy with the arrangement, but perhaps that was because Dawn had spent so much time at Izzy's house.

Breathing in the sharp smell of fresh paint, Izzy stretched out an arm to ring the bell and at the same moment the door came open and she realised the man who stood there must have been watching her through the net curtains.

'Yes?' He had a small round head and very little hair. His cheeks were like two soft pouches and his full lips gave him a slightly effeminate appearance.

'I'm sorry to bother you,' Izzy said, 'but I'm looking for Mrs Dear.'

'What was it you wanted?'

'My name's Isabel Lomas. I went to school with her daughter.'

'With Dawn? You're a friend of Dawn's?' He turned to call back into the house. 'Rosalie, come quick, we've a visitor.'

Rosalie Dear came down the passage, drying her hands on a towel, and as she drew closer Izzy noticed she had a slightly wild-eyed look. She stared at Izzy for a moment as though she could hardly believe what she was seeing then her shoulders relaxed and she was back in control of herself.

'Izzy, what a surprise.' She turned to the man who was now hovering behind her. 'It's Sylvia's girl, Francis. When we lived in Chester.'

'I've been visiting a friend in the Lake District,' Izzy lied. 'When I realised how close to you I was, I decided to make a diversion.'

'You haven't changed.'

'Nor have you.' It wasn't true, but what else could she say? And who was Francis?

'Come in then.' Rosalie spoke sharply but that was always her way. 'Are you still living in Exeter?'

'Yes, yes I am.'

'Married?'

'No.'

'But living with someone, I expect. Your mother – how's she bearing up? I wrote to her – after it happened. Your father was always so kind, you must miss him.'

They were standing in a small room at the front of the house. The clock on the mantelpiece had a particularly loud tick – Izzy remembered it from the flat in Chester – and accentuated the tension between them. Francis tried to break it with a remark about the weather, but Rosalie ignored him.

'Where's Dawn?' she asked, and then because the question had sounded so blunt. 'She wrote to me and told me she and Miles were coming back from Portugal but since then I've heard nothing.'

'Nor me. Actually I was hoping you might know where

26

she is.'

The man called Francis put an arm round Rosalie's shoulder. 'I'm afraid it may be my fault. When Rosalie told Dawn about ... about me and her mother, she didn't take it well.' He gazed at Rosalie, willing her to contradict him but she was silent, grim-faced, so he turned to Izzy instead.

'Sit yourself down and I'll make a pot of tea. The two of you will have so much to catch up on and maybe if you put your heads together ...'

Rosalie's fingers drummed on the windowsill. 'You met Miles, I expect, what's he like?'

'I only saw him once.'

'Why did they go to Portugal?'

'I'm not sure.' So Rosalie knew even less than she did. 'I suppose they wanted to get right away.'

'Yes, I thought it must something like that. He's married?'

'Dawn didn't tell you?'

Rosalie frowned. 'And you haven't heard anything for the last six or seven months?'

'No.'

They sat in uncomfortable silence, listening to Francis clattering about in the kitchen, then Rosalie stood up and began talking while keeping her back turned. 'Dawn didn't tell you about Francis then? No, it's all right, I could see from your face. We met when he did some work for me on the house. Well, that's what I say to people, although in truth I knew his father years ago, when Francis was in his teens. We're not married.'

When Izzy said nothing, Rosalie gave a small shrug and continued. 'I'm only telling you because now you'll wonder why I object to what Dawn's done, only it's not conventions I'm interested in, I just don't like people getting hurt. I assume this Miles character walked out on his wife. Were there any children?'

'I don't think so.'

'That's something I suppose.' She was looking at her watch, shaking her wrist as though she thought it must have gone wrong. She had put on weight and it had the effect of making her look less tall than Izzy remembered, but no less intimidating. Her hair had turned grey and frizzy and her face was deeply lined. Somehow Izzy had expected her to look more or less the same age as her own mother, which was absurd since Rosalie must be at least fifteen years older.

In the past, she had worn contact lenses, which Izzy had believed accounted for the fact that she blinked such a lot. Now she wore glasses but the blinking was the same as ever. 'I wouldn't want to give the impression Dawn and I have fallen out,' she said, 'I was sorry when she gave up her work at the university but she knows I'd stand by her whatever she did. After all those years with the cult I'd got used to not seeing her very often, but when she returned to her studies I had hopes.'

Francis pushed open the door with his shoulder and placed a tray on a table under the window. 'Made any progress?' he asked, 'fitted any pieces into the jigsaw?'

'I'm afraid not.' Izzy was thinking how her father had often joked about Rosalie being such a snob. Francis, with his strong local accent, seemed to contradict all that. She guessed he was a fair bit younger than Rosalie, who would now be old enough to draw a pension. At one time, Dawn had said something about her mother working in a cheese factory, but only to tide her over until she found something better.

Francis was passing round the cups of tea. Rosalie put hers on the mantelpiece then began straightening the ornaments. 'Dawn gave away everything she owned,' she said, 'it was the policy of the cult. I thought it was the end. I thought she'd stay there forever.'

'Yes, I did too.' For the first time, Izzy felt sorry for Rosalie. She had never liked her very much but having your only child join a religious cult would be tough.

'She was always a one for grand gestures. When she left the cult, she became an avid atheist. Did you know that? Flipped from one extreme to the other.'

'We never talked about it much, apart from her interest in theology.'

'An academic interest,' Rosalie said, sounding quite proud of her daughter. 'I don't think one's required to be a believer. You'll stay for something to eat. Won't be anything special, I'm afraid, just cold meat and salad.'

'Thank you, but I think I ought to start back quite soon. It's a long drive even though most it's motorway.'

Rosalie made no comment. She was disappointed, not because Izzy's visit was to be so short but because there was no news of Dawn. The trip had been a waste of time. Izzy had learned nothing, apart from the mildly interesting fact that Rosalie had invited her handyman to move in with her. And that Dawn knew about it but had chosen not to tell her. Because she disapproved? She ought to be glad her mother was no longer on her own. On second thoughts, perhaps the journey had been worthwhile after all. Surely if Dawn had been pregnant she would have told her mother. Only … perhaps not.

'Stuart Robbins,' Rosalie said, 'you've met him, I expect.'

'I don't think so.'

'He works in Exeter. He's a naturalist, connected to the university, studies birds. That's why Dawn chose it, I imagine, so there would be someone to pull strings, help

29

her obtain her scholarship. His parents lived here when Dawn was a small child, the house on the front, two doors down from the café. He was back not long ago, to settle his parents' estate. They died within a few months of each other.'

'Always the best way.' Francis glanced at Rosalie and cleared his throat again. 'If you know what I mean.'

'I don't think Dawn mentioned him.' Izzy stood up and Rosalie was unable to disguise her relief. Then, as if to make up for it, she clasped both of her hands.

'If you hear from Dawn, you will ask her to get in touch?'

'Yes of course. I expect she and Miles changed their minds, decided to stay on in Portugal. Dawn was never very good at writing letters, was she?'

'Did you meet the wife?'

'No, by the time Dawn introduced him to me, Miles was living in a rented room.'

'Where's your car parked?' Francis pushed back his chair. 'I'll walk down the road with you if that's all right, could do with a breath of air.'

Rosalie gave Izzy a stiff little hug. 'So nice to see you after all this time. We haven't talked nearly enough about you. Are you well? You look tired but I expect that's the drive. You must come again. You will come.'

'Yes I'd like that.'

'And do give my best to your mother.'

'She's in New Zealand, staying with Dan and his family, but she'll be back at the end of the month.'

It had started to drizzle. Francis zipped up his brown anorak, pulling the hood over his head and tying a bow under his chin, and together they set off in the direction of the sea front.

At the end of the terrace, he paused. 'Fresh air's an

excuse, Izzy. You don't mind if I call you Izzy? Only I wanted a quick word – it's about Dawn's father. I wondered how much you knew.'

'Hardly anything except his name was Graham. Dawn had a photo of him she kept in a copy of *The Railway Children*. It was her favourite book. Actually it's only occurred to me recently, I never knew why he died.'

'An accident. Faulty piece of equipment in the clothing factory. I couldn't tell you the details.'

'But Dawn's father was a salesman. I remember that much.'

'Is that right?' The wind blew rain in their faces. With his hood covering everything except his eyes and nose, Francis had a slightly sinister appearance. 'I learned all I know from Lorraine at the teashop. Rosalie used to chat to her, after she moved back from Chester, not that the woman had lived here when Dawn was a child.'

'Rosalie never talks to you about Graham?'

He shook his head. 'Her first love,' he said sadly, 'nothing like it, is there?'

What was he telling her? That Rosalie was unable to commit herself because of a man who had died more than twenty years ago?

'You're sure you've no idea where she is?' He clutched at Izzy's arm. 'Only Rosalie frets so. I wanted us to get married, do things properly, but she won't think of it, not until she's sure ...' His voice trembled with emotion. 'Until she's sure her Dawn's still alive.'

3

Somehow Josh had found out about the baby.

'I won't stay long.' He took hold of Izzy's shoulders and pushed past her into the house, 'I had to make sure you were OK.'

'Why wouldn't I be?'

'Well ...' He tried to think of a reason. 'It must have been a bit of a surprise. What happened exactly? You opened the front door and –'

'She was crying. It was the middle of the night.'

Josh whistled through his teeth. 'Have they traced the mother? Dave bumped into Kath at the supermarket and she couldn't wait to tell him. Probably the most exciting thing that's happened to her for years.'

Izzy gave a brief account of Fairbrother's visit, and how the baby had been placed with foster parents in Dawlish, but by then Josh had lost interest and started talking about himself.

'I'm a reformed character, Izzy. No, really. Time to stop behaving like an overgrown schoolboy and make a go of my life. I've persuaded my boss to give me a more or less free hand with the latest contract and I reckon he's going to be impressed.'

As he expanded on his bigger and better plans, Izzy listened sufficiently to make the occasional non-committal comment but most of her attention was focussed on how it felt to have him sitting there. She had always been a sucker for good looks. It was a mistake. Find someone who shares the same interests so when the initial attraction wears off you can still enjoy each other's company. All passion spent, a nice reliable friend who would never let you down.

'What are you thinking?' Josh smiled. The same smile that had once turned her knees to jelly.

'I'm tired. We've had a rush on at work, a project that has to be completed by the end of the week.'

'Right.' He ran his hand down Blanche's back, making her purr with pleasure. 'So Blanche hasn't been pining away without me. Fickle as hell. That's what comes from getting a female.'

He was chewing the nail on his little finger, a habit he found impossible to give up. 'Pity you couldn't sell your story to the papers,' he said, 'only I expect abandoned babies are two a penny. I'll open a bottle of wine, shall I, or would that be breaking the rules?'

Out in the kitchen, taking glasses from the cupboard, he continued to talk. 'God I've missed you. I said, I've missed you.'

'I heard.'

'What about you?' He returned with the wine. 'I suppose your main feeling's been one of relief.'

'How's Dave?' She wanted to know if Josh was still staying in his flat but a direct question might be interpreted as a suggestion they give it another go.

'Dave's fine.' He had broken the cork, something he considered a deadly sin. 'See what you've made me do.

No, it's all right I'm not going to say anything about "us". One quick drink and I'll be on my way. Late showing at the film society, some Italian movie, not really my kind of thing but Dave's got these actor friends.' He sat down, burying his head in his hands. 'I'm only blathering on because I feel so fucking awful.'

After he left, she started cleaning the cooker. Hard manual labour was the only antidote. It was so typical. Telling her how much he missed her then just happening to mention how he had a pleasant evening ahead of him. Then one final wail of self-pity. Why had he come round? Because he was genuinely concerned or out of curiosity so he could tell Dave and his 'actor friends' about the abandoned baby – about Cressy. What difference did it make? It was over between them. Asking him to leave had taken every ounce of strength she possessed and she had no intention of putting herself in a position where she had to go through it all over again. Sod him. Sod everyone. When she got up in the morning she had found one of his socks in her drawer. Had he left it there on purpose – to remind her? What went on in his head or did he just live from moment to moment? Once they had been happy. Or she had. Once.

DS Fairbrother phoned to say the foster parents would be happy for Izzy to visit the baby.

Izzy wrote down the address and phone number. 'Thanks, I'll give them a call.'

'Bev and Alan Jordan,' Fairbrother told her, 'they're also fostering a thirteen-year-old boy and a twelve-year-old girl but those kids are long term. Hopefully the baby's mother will come forward in a week or two.'

Now was the moment she ought to tell her. But what? It was too soon, she had no proof. What could she say? By

35

the way, a friend of mine – well, she used to be friend only I haven't seen her for over a year … It's probably nothing but once, years ago, when we were still at primary school we used to play this game …

She needed to see the baby. Did she look like Dawn? Tens of thousands of babies had the same fair colouring, the same round surprised-looking eyes, and how on earth could the person who had been her childhood friend, so close they could have been sisters, have abandoned her baby?

Dawn Dear. Top of the class. Good at just about everything apart from sport, popular with teachers and pupils alike. But there had been another side to her, a side only Izzy, and perhaps Rosalie, had known about. An angry, vindictive side that could be turned on anyone who thwarted her or – if she thought she deserved it – turned harshly, mercilessly, against herself.

The drive to Dawlish would take less than an hour. During the day, Izzy had phoned the university on the off-chance that Dawn might have been in touch with her old department. The woman who answered the phone was reluctant to pass on any information, then relented and said they had heard nothing from Dawn since she sent a brief note to let them know she was going to Portugal. Did Izzy know if and when she would be returning? Her supervisor needed to speak to her – this probably meant she had failed to pay her tuition fees – but had no means of getting in touch.

'I'm sorry. I'm trying to locate her myself.'

'I see. Well, if you succeed, I'd be grateful if you'd tell her we need to speak to her.'

Izzy had never asked Dawn why she had chosen to come to this particular university. Because someone on the staff shared her interest in a branch of theology, or because she knew Izzy lived in the city?

Ten years ago, when they were both nineteen, she had joined Dawn in London, but they had never lived together. Expecting Dawn, who was in her second year, to have her own friends, Izzy had arranged to share with three other students from her art college. When Dawn found out she had been angry; not that she had expressed her feelings openly, but Izzy knew her well enough to be aware of her resentment.

Later, Dawn had moved into a room close to where Izzy was living, but only for six months. As soon as her course finished, even before she had the result of her exams – although it was a foregone conclusion she would get a First – she had announced she was going to Scotland to join a community. At first, Izzy had thought she intended to become a nun, as her mother had once wanted, but it wasn't that kind of community although it appeared Dawn had to give up all her worldly goods, whatever that amounted to.

For a long time there had been no word from her, then a letter had arrived saying how blissfully happy she was, only to be followed by a silence that had lasted nearly two years. Izzy had written twice and sent a card on Dawn's birthday, wondering, as she wrote in it, if cards were permitted or counted as personal possessions. Then, a few months after she started her present job, Dawn had written saying she was in the process of putting her life back together and would be starting a research degree in Exeter in the not too distant future ...

After a grey, dreary start to the day, the weather had suddenly cleared. From the top of the hill, Izzy could see the sea. She liked Dawlish, with its famous black swans, and the railway line that ran parallel to the beach so that the mainline trains were sometimes splashed by waves in the winter months.

Bev Jordan had told her to ignore the sign pointing to the town centre and carry straight on until she passed two sets of traffic lights. After that she had to turn right, then take the second on the left, then right again.

It was a part of the town she had never visited before, newish houses interspersed with small open spaces. No thatched cottages here. She passed a play area where children – most of them too large for the equipment – were running up slides or standing on swings. It was starting to get dark and she had lost her bearings, thought she must have turned off too soon, then she passed the end of a street and spotted the name she was looking for.

Bev and Alan Jordan's house was a square redbrick box with a white front door. No climbing plants or shrubs, nothing to differentiate it from the houses on either side. Izzy rang the bell, in the knowledge it was unnecessary since a teenage boy was watching her through a downstairs window.

A moment later he greeted her with a smile, holding the door to let her pass and then preceding her into a living room that ran from the front of the house to the back. The room had an overhead light with a large paper shade, and two table lamps, both with purple shades and red bases. Bookshelves set into alcoves on either side of the fireplace were piled high with jigsaw puzzles, boxes containing board games, and copies of a weekly magazine designed to build into an encyclopaedia of British wildlife.

Someone was coming down the stairs. Izzy assumed it would be Bev Jordan but it turned out to be an old dog with a long shaggy body and a fiercely wagging tail.

'He's all right,' the boy told her, 'but if you don't like dogs I'll put him in the kitchen.'

'No, he's fine. I have a cat, but I like dogs too.

'I expect he can smell your cat.'

'Yes, I expect so.' Izzy bent to stroke the dog's head, watching as he ambled away, sniffing the carpet before settling down behind an armchair with his nose resting on his paws. The room smelled of dogs. Their owners get so used to it the smell no longer registers. Cats didn't smell, at least she was fairly sure they didn't.

'Isabel!' Bev Jordan's greeting made Izzy feel like a long-lost friend. 'How lovely to meet you.'

A large, fair-haired woman, she was wearing jeans that were slightly too short and a pale blue, much-washed sweatshirt, and her round pleasant face couldn't have been more friendly. Although there was something about her eyes, sadness, or was it worry?

'Cressy's asleep,' she said, 'but she'll wake quite soon. She's settled in beautifully, poor little love, such a contented baby. Isn't it strange how a child who's had all the care and attention in the world lavished on it can be miserable and colicky and one like Cressy ...' She broke off. 'I'm so pleased you could come. The social worker seemed to think it a little odd you wanting to visit. All that training they go through – I sometimes think the only effect is to knock their native common sense and normal human feelings out of them. In your position I'd have felt exactly the same. Oh, I'm sorry.' She glanced at the girl who had crept into the room. 'I always talk too much don't I, Pippa? Has Nigel introduced himself? Alan, my husband, had to go out but he should be back any time. Do sit down, Isabel.'

Izzy joined Pippa on the sofa. 'Most people call me Izzy.'

'Izzy. Good. And I'm Bev, short for Beverley. I don't know what my parents were thinking about.'

'No news about the mother then?'

Bev shook her head. 'Apparently they've been trying to trace where the carrycot was bought but so far they've drawn a blank – and with so many possibilities it seems a bit of a lost cause. The mother could have answered an ad in one of those papers that advertise second-hand stuff. I wonder if she had any more baby clothes. No, it's all right, I bought what I needed – social services take care of the cost – and we found some stuff in a charity shop, didn't we, Pippa? Coffee or would you prefer tea?'

'Nothing for me, thanks.' In spite of Bev's welcome, Izzy was starting to wonder why she had come. Being the person who found the baby gave her no particular rights. Cressy would be brought down, she would hold her briefly, check surreptitiously for any likeness to Dawn, exchange a few pleasantries with the Jordans, and leave.

'She's a lovely baby,' Bev was saying, 'such beautiful eyes and all that hair. Quite unusual-looking. I suppose the mother could be a foreigner, Scandinavian or something, although come to think of it, the father might be the fair one. Nigel and Pippa are ever so good with her. The trouble is, when they find the mother we're all going to miss her horribly.'

Pippa let out a long dramatic sigh. 'If they don't, can we keep her?'

'Oh Pippa, I explained, it's no good getting too attached. Let's just make the most of her while she's here.' Bev glanced at her watch. 'Can't think what's happened to Alan. He wanted to meet you, Izzy, and I told him what time you were coming.'

A small sound came from upstairs and in an instant Nigel had jumped to his feet. 'My turn,' he said, pushing Pippa out of the way. 'It is my turn, isn't it, Bev?'

So they called her Bev. Izzy wondered about their

40

background. By their looks, she guessed they were brother and sister, not just two separate children who had ended up with the same foster parents. What had happened to their real parents? She had gained the impression they had been living with Bev for some time.

Nigel raced up the stairs with Pippa following.

'Don't worry,' Bev said, 'they're ever so careful, wouldn't dream of fighting when it comes to lifting her out of the cot.' She lowered her voice. 'Their Dad died three years ago and their Mum's been in and out of psychiatric hospital. Nigel's thirteen – he's the quiet one – and Pippa's twelve. They see their mother on a fairly regular basis – when she's well enough she takes them out for the day – but there's very little chance she'll ever be able to make a home for them, and they're settled here, I doubt if they'd want to be uprooted again.'

'No, I'm sure.' Izzy was thinking how it was not surprising there was always a shortage of foster parents. What must it be like? Kids coming and going, attachments formed then broken. Presumably Bev was unable to have her own children. How did it feel looking after Cressy in the knowledge that any day the police – or the social worker – could give her a ring to let her know the natural mother wanted to reclaim her?

Nigel and Pippa were coming down the stairs. Nigel was carrying Cressy, and Pippa was carrying her blanket. Izzy felt an absurd twinge of jealousy, almost as if they had stolen her baby.

'I chose her blanket, didn't I, Bev?'

'You did.'

'People always give girl babies pink things but I read in a book they like stripes and red is my favourite colour.'

'Give her to Izzy,' Bev said, 'I'll go and heat her bottle.'

'Not it's all right.' she patted the sofa. 'You keep her, Nigel. I'll hold her in a minute or two.'

Nigel and Pippa exchanged glances. Pippa started to say something then broke off blushing.

'She wants to know where you found her.' Nigel shifted the baby's weight from one arm to the other. 'We know it was outside your house but was it in the garage or something?'

'I haven't got a garage and the house opens straight onto the street, but it's pedestrianized, no cars allowed. I was lying in bed. Her crying woke me but at first I thought it was a cat. Then she started to cry properly.'

'Was she all cold and wet?' Pippa asked. 'It's a funny name – Cressy. Bev says it must be short for Cressida. I've never heard of anyone called Cressida, have you?'

'No.' Izzy stretched out her arms and Nigel handed her the baby. 'She's lucky she's come to stay with you, lucky to have so many people taking care of her.'

Pippa gave a nervous giggle. 'But not lucky her mother doesn't want her.'

Nigel dug his sister in the ribs with his elbow. 'You don't know that. She could be ill or in trouble with the police. It's not like she hadn't been looked after.'

Bev had returned with the bottle. She handed it to Izzy, along with a small white cloth. 'To catch the drips,' she explained, 'she's not a sicky baby but she does tend to suck rather too hard.'

'Greedy guzzler,' said Pippa, springing up when she heard a key in the front door. 'Alan, the lady that found Cressy is here. She thought she was a cat.'

Alan Jordan was a tall, well-built man with curly brown hair and deep lines between his eyes. He held out a hand to Izzy then withdrew it, apologizing for the dirt. 'Been helping a friend put his fence back up. Wind brought it down a couple of nights back.'

'Alan's a telephone engineer,' Bev explained, 'but I work at home, on my word processor, although I've cut down on it since Cressy arrived. You're an artist, is that right?'

'I work for a graphics company.'

'I'm going to be an artist,' chimed in Pippa, 'and Nigel's going to be an aeroplane designer.'

Alan laughed. 'Then he'll have to start playing less football and doing more schoolwork.'

'Oh come on,' Bev protested, 'that's not very fair.' She put an arm round Nigel's shoulder. 'Do me a favour, love, run down the end and buy a large granary.'

Alan was watching Izzy closely and she wondered if he found it a little odd that she had wanted to see Cressy again. 'Must've been a shock,' he said.

'Finding the baby? Yes, it was.'

'Any idea why she was left outside your house?'

'No.' So did he too suspect it had been chosen specially? 'There's a porch, part of a porch. Enough to keep the rain off the carry cot.'

He thought about this and she guessed he thought it an improbable explanation. 'I expect you're right. Wonder what's happened to the mother. Expect she'll turn up sooner or later.'

'Yes.' Izzy was starting to feel uneasy and Bev picked this up and quickly changed the subject.

'You work in Exeter, do you?'

'Yes, that's right. Our office is down near the river. Lots of glass. Too hot in summer and too cold in winter.' The baby was spluttering and Izzy handed her to Bev, who put Cressy up against her shoulder and patted her back.

'Told you she was a greedy guzzler. Putting on weight and the health visitor says she's doing well. Perfect.

Perfect little girl.'

'Am I a perfect little girl?' Pippa asked.

Bev and Alan both answered together.

'Of course,' Bev said.

'Too naughty,' Alan laughed.

'No, I'm not. I'm not, am I, Bev?'

Bev gave Izzy a sympathetic smile. 'I'm so glad you came.'

'Thank you. So am I.'

Pippa was nudging Izzy. 'I want a cat but Alan says they have fleas, but they don't if you look after them properly.'

'Shhh, Pippa.' Alan frowned at her. 'You talk too much.'

'No, I don't. I don't, do I, Bev?'

Izzy decided it was time to leave. She had intended the visit to be a one-off, but as she walked towards her car, Bev insisted she must drop by again. 'You can give me a ring if you like but I'm never out for long, unless I've popped to the supermarket or taken the baby for a walk. '

'I'd call first,' Izzy said, wondering if she would. 'Thanks. Oh, Bev, it's nothing to do with me, but are Pippa and Nigel full sister and brother?'

'Yes, that's right, didn't I tell you? They try not to split up families. I'm so glad we were able to foster them both. They fight sometimes, but I'm sure all brothers and sisters are the same. When they first arrived, Nigel was very protective of Pippa, but he's given all that up now. I hope it means they both feel safe and secure.'

'I'm sure they do.' Izzy would like to have known more about their background. But not now. Next time she visited perhaps.

'Good to meet you.' Bev kissed her on the cheek. 'Come back whenever you like.'

44

As she drove off, Izzy's head was reeling. What had she expected to find? Suddenly Bev and her family had become important to her, comforting. She could never tell Bev what she suspected. Even so, she looked forward to seeing her again.

Did Cressy look like Dawn or was she imagining it?

Oh, Dawn, where you? And at the thought of her one-time friend, a shiver of fear ran down her back.

Back home, Kath was waiting on the doorstep and she remembered with a guilty pang that it was Thursday, the day they always went out for a drink together.

'Thought you'd forgotten.' Kath sounded put out. 'Where've you been? Are we still on?'

'Yes of course. Sorry. I've been to see the baby's foster parents and I didn't mean to stay so long. They're a really nice family, two teenage kids, a boy and a girl, and they both seem to like babies.'

'And the parents?' Kath accompanied Izzy into the house.

'Bev and Alan. Very friendly. Look, do you want to go out or shall I open a bottle?'

'Suits me. You look whacked. These foster parents – tell me more. They've been doing it a long time, have they? It must take a special kind of person, wouldn't you say? Imagine getting fond of a baby then –'

'Kath?' Izzy called from the kitchen. 'You know I was brought up in Chester.'

'Chester? Sure. Not that I've been there. We must visit some time and you can show me the house.'

'The thing is ...' Returning with two glasses, Izzy hesitated, wondering if confiding in Kath was a good idea or if it would mean two people instead of one ended up withholding information from the police?

'Were you born in hospital?' Kath was asking. 'I came into the world in the back of an old Chevy.'

'Really? Why? What happened?'

'Couldn't tell you exactly. Might not be right, although I guess the story always had a ring of truth about it. My mother had a way of embroidering things, taking an ounce of reality and building it up into a jaw-dropping saga. She didn't want me but she wouldn't give me up for adoption. That way you get the worst of all possible worlds: kids' home, couple of temporary placements, then, when I was eleven, she took one of her regular overdoses and this time made a better job of it.'

'Oh Kath, I'm so sorry.' Izzy was shocked. 'And all the time I thought you had a family in Ohio.'

'Because that's what I wanted you to think. Everything else was true. Meeting Jim when he was on holiday in the States, getting married, coming to live over here, getting a divorce.'

'What about your father?'

Kath shrugged. 'Doubt if my mother knew which one he was.'

'So all this stuff with the baby – with Cressy – must have stirred up memories. There was me thinking I'd had such a traumatic experience and all the time …'

Kath patted her on the shoulder. 'How is the baby? Doing well I expect? Tough little buggers, babies, need to be that way I guess.'

4

Where was Dawn now? With Miles, or had they split up? He could have returned to his wife. And left her with the baby? Izzy had only met him once, very briefly, and knew nothing about him, but first impressions are often correct and she had wondered at the time how he would handle Dawn's unpredictable moods and determination to get her own way. Possibly, his wife was equally determined and he had been caught in middle of two women wanting him to live with them. He could have run away, disappeared. No, what was the use of trying to work out what had happened? It was all so frustrating. And not just that. The thought of DS Fairbrother loomed large in Izzy's mind.

Blanche had gone through the cat flap and was still out, unless she had slipped back into the house without Izzy noticing. The garden was so small the cat usually scaled the wall straight away and Izzy lived in dread she would be killed crossing the main road. All through her childhood, she and her two older brothers had never been without a collection of pets. A dog, a cat, plus numerous hamsters that had the advantage they could live in your bedroom but the disadvantage they had a lifespan of only a couple of years. A corner of the garden was reserved as a burial place, with crosses made out of ice-lolly sticks and names written in felt pen that faded in the sun. After Pushkin was found dead, she had wanted to know why, wanted a post-mortem, but her mother said the vet thought the cat must have eaten weedkiller. At the time, Izzy had accepted the explanation but later it occurred to her that cats were fussy about what they ate – unless someone deliberately put poison in their food.

There was no sign of Blanche in the garden. Izzy strolled down the road, looking in front gardens and between houses. Then she tried the patch of grass, surrounded by trees, but the only cat she spotted was a Siamese one, sharpening its claws on the wooden seat. Because it was pedestrianized, it was a relatively safe road but the trouble with cats: unlike dogs, they were territorial and liked to inspect the surrounding area. Izzy called Blanche's name a few times then returned to the house, jumping back, almost as if she had come face to face with an intruder.

During the brief time she had been away, a package had been propped against her front door, bound up with sticky tape. Who had left it? Surely whoever it was must still be around? Izzy ran to the end of the opposite road and screwed up her eyes, staring into the distance, but there was no one in sight.

Tearing the parcel open, she found a sheet of lined paper wrapped round a white teddy bear, dressed in a navy blue jumper with a picture of a boat on the front. A gift from a well-wisher? When a baby was found abandoned, hospitals were inundated with toys – she had read about it in the paper – but Fairbrother had reassured her no one knew her address, although it was possible someone in the street had seen the police with the carrycot, and put two and two together. Who was she fooling? Wishful thinking – it had to be.

The lined paper had been written on in red. Block capitals so badly formed they looked as though the sender had used his or her 'wrong' hand.

YOU MUST GET HER BACK, she read. YOU'RE SUPPOSED TO BE LOOKING AFTER HER. BE CAREFUL WHAT YOU DO OR YOU COULD LAND YOURSELF IN SERIOUS DANGER. OR FIND YOURSELF RESPONSIBLE FOR A DEATH.

Blanche had returned and was busy kneading the crackly brown paper the bear had been wrapped in. Izzy stared at it, with its missing fur and beady glass eyes, and pictured it as she had first seen it, standing looking out of the window of the first floor flat in Elwood Road. As far as she knew it had never been taken to bed, perhaps because it was too small, but in any case, Dawn had been the least sentimental child Izzy had ever met.

Harry was in his office, checking the messages on his phone.

'Izzy.' His revolving chair spun round and she saw he had a half-eaten bar of chocolate in his hand. 'How are you? All the hoo-ha about the changeling died down, I hope. Apparently there are one or two cases a week, but we only hear about a handful of them.'

'I went to see the foster family.' Izzy sat on the arm of one of the pair of new leather chairs Harry had bought to impress clients. 'They live in Dawlish, on an estate.'

'Really? Wasn't that a bit beyond the call of duty?'

'I wanted to make sure she was all right. Actually, if I'm honest I suppose I just wanted to see her.'

'Yes, I think I understand.' Harry's voice was softer than usual, in fact his whole manner was quieter, more thoughtful. 'Anyway you look refreshed from your weekend trip. Good idea to get away. Amazing how a change of scene puts your life into a different frame.'

'That wasn't the reason I went, Harry. Do you remember me talking about someone I'd known as a child in Chester? Dawn Dear – she came here to do a Ph.D. in theology.'

'What is she – a female vicar?'

'No, nothing like that. She went through a phase of being a fanatical believer in something or other, spent time with a community in Scotland, then suddenly left.'

'Saw the light?' Harry was starting to take an interest. 'Does all this have something to do with the abandoned baby?'

'No, I'm sure it doesn't. Before her mother came to Chester she'd been living in the Wirral and that's where her mother's returned.'

'Hang on. You went all that way to see your friend's mother? Why?'

'I was worried about Dawn, wanted to find out where she is now, but her mother had no more idea than I did. Or if she did, she wasn't going to let on. While I was there, she told me about someone called Stuart Robbins. I wondered if you'd come across him. He'd met Dawn but didn't know her well. He lives in Exeter, does research into sea birds, but he's interested in history too. Only, you're interested in old churches, aren't you?'

Harry laughed, running his hands through his new haircut. 'Old churches – do you mind? Victorian architecture and I'm quite an aficionado I'll have you know. Yes, I know Robbins. Not well but I went to a lecture he gave. Interesting chap. We had a drink together after the lecture.' He paused, closing his eyes and leaning back in his chair. 'I haven't talked to him recently but I've heard ... No, it doesn't matter.'

'What? What have you heard?' But he wasn't going to tell her and it was unlikely to have anything to do with Dawn.

'Dawn had this boyfriend – called Miles. He was married, but when I met him he'd left his wife, moved into a bedsit. I'm going to look up his wife.'

'Are you sure that's a good idea?' Harry was starting to become suspicious. 'You sound as though you're taking too much on yourself. Surely if you have any suspicions at all, the police should –'

'No, I can't.'

He waited for an explanation.

'I mean, I will tell them, but not just yet. Miles' address is still in the phone book. There's only one entry for Bruton, M so it's worth a try.'

Harry stood up. 'I'm starting to worry about you, Izzy. The way you're going things could easily get out of hand. Why did you want to know about Stuart Robbins? You think … No, it can't be that.'

'I just thought he might know where Dawn is now. Forget it, you're right. A wild goose chase. I should leave it to the police.'

'But tell them everything you know.'

'Yes, of course.'

He looked at her, doubtfully. 'I'm sorry about Josh. It must have been a wrench. No regrets?'

'No.' So he thought she was acting irrationally, as a diversion from her own problems.

'If you want to meet Robbins I'll see what I can do, but only on the understanding you keep me posted on what you're up to. I worry about you, Izzy, we all do. You've been looking exhausted lately.'

'I'm still getting my work done.'

'Of course. I've no complaints in that department.'

51

In the summer, she and Josh had walked on the dunes at Dawlish Warren, a little farther along the coast. The beach stretched as far as the Exe estuary and part of the area was a nature reserve, enjoyed by bird watchers. Wading birds could be seen from a hide – either side of high tide was the best time – and rare birds sometimes landed when the weather was bad, normally between August and mid-November.

Izzy was thinking about the man called Stuart Robbins, who worked at the university and studied birds. Josh had no interest in birds, but Izzy liked to watch them and she loved the way the seagulls dropped the heavy shells of clams and mussels onto rocks in order to eat the contents.

Had Stuart Robbins known Dawn well? She had no recollection of her mentioning his name, but that meant nothing. Perhaps she *should* contact him – she could say the university wanted to get in touch with Dawn – but perhaps not since it might complicate the situation even more. The fewer people involved, the better, although Izzy longed to confide in someone and ask their advice.

'How goes it?'

DS Fairbrother strode into the house as if she owned it. She was wearing a grey jacket which she removed and hung over the back of a chair, revealing a red top made out of some velvety material and black trousers stretched tightly over her substantial thighs.

'Been to see the nipper?' she asked, making it clear the question was rhetorical. 'There's always a shortage of foster parents. Social Service have been having a recruitment drive but without a great deal of success.'

'The Jordans seem a very nice family.'

'Good.' Fairbrother was so relaxed, Izzy was starting to think it was a social call, although wouldn't that be carrying the wish to promote good relations between police and public a bit too far? Of course, it could be a trap. Up to now, Izzy had believed police officers worked in pairs. Had they selected a woman, and let her visit on her own, to lull her into a false sense of security, make her think Fairbrother was her friend.

'Coffee?' she asked, but Fairbrother shook her head.

'No thanks. The last time I was here ... after I'd gone ... my fault entirely but a couple of questions came up and I wondered if you'd be able to help.'

'What questions?' Immediately Izzy was on her guard.

Fairbrother paused before answering, building up the tension, increasing Izzy's anxiety. 'The main one that came to mind – you said you thought the baby must have been left outside your house because of the piece of overhanging roof.'

'The old porch. It needs pulling down. I keep meaning to do it but –'

'But some of the houses farther down have complete porches. Wouldn't she have been safer under one of them?'

'Not if the mother came from ... I've no idea which way she'd have come. I expect she chose the first suitable spot.'

'Not if the mother came from the opposite direction? Is that what you were going to say?'

'Yes. No. I was just thinking aloud. As I said before, I expect she thought the pedestrianized part was safest.'

Fairbrother made a few notes. 'None of your friends have recently given birth?'

'No.'

'Relatives?'

'My mother's in New Zealand, visiting my eldest brother. My other brother's gay.'

'I see.' Fairbrother stared at her for a few moments, as though she expected more, and Izzy was afraid her response had come too easily, as though she had invented a cover story and rehearsed what she was going to say.

'Just one thing more.' Fairbrother smiled at her but Izzy didn't smile back. 'This may seem an odd question, but why did you want to see the baby again?'

'I told you, I wanted to make sure she was all right. Poor little thing, she was so hungry. I heated her bottle of milk, made it too hot, then had to cool it down. I felt so sorry for her. Imagine being –'

'Sure. I get it. Meeting up in a crisis forms a special attachment, like people who get stuck in a broken-down lift.'

Izzy said nothing. She had heard the theory before, something about mutual fear, adrenalin. As far as possible, she avoided lifts, but sometimes it was impossible. Crushed together, with a group of uncongenial people, it was hard to imagine a special bond developing. Not that she had a phobia about lifts, nor about anything else. Apart from the mud at the estuary, and a fear of sinking into deep mud was perfectly rational, as was a fear of falling off a high cliff.

Blanche had come downstairs and seeing a visitor made a beeline for her lap. Fairbrother reached out a hand to stroke the cat's head then placed her on a chair and stood up to study the photograph of Izzy and Josh on holiday in France. 'The name Cressy – did it ring any bells?'

'Why should it?' But her reply had come out too quickly, sounded too definite.

Fairbrother gave her a sharp glance. 'Well, I think that's all for now.'

For now? But if Fairbrother's suspicions had been aroused she showed no sign of it. Now was the time to tell her about the parcel, particularly the teddy bear with the navy blue jumper, but if she did that she would have to tell her everything.

A fleeting smile crossed Fairbrother's face. 'No, don't bother to come to the front door, I'll let myself out. Will you be visiting the Jordans again?'

'I'm not sure. Bev said she was happy for me to call round whenever I liked but it might seem ... I'm thinking about it.'

Fairbrother nodded. 'Odd place to leave your baby. Most people choose a hospital or shopping centre.'

Izzy was silent. Anything she said made her feel like she was digging a bigger and bigger hole. But the silence was incriminating too. She knew now how people felt when they were accused of a crime they hadn't committed. Withholding information was a crime, wasn't it – but she had no definite information and it would be equally irresponsible to send the police off on a pointless search.

Who was she fooling? Certainly not herself. But there was something about Fairbrother that made her want to keep quiet a little longer. Then what would she do? She could pretend the name Cressy had only just triggered off a memory from long ago. Fairbrother wouldn't believe her but neither would she be able to prove it was a lie.

'As I said, any news and I'll be in touch.'

'Yes. Thanks.' Izzy surprised herself with how unperturbed she sounded.

'Although if you and Bev Jordan have hit it off so well I daresay she'll be the one to let you know if and when we trace the mother.'

Did that mean it was the last she was going to see of the police? After Fairbrother left, Izzy poured herself a glass of wine and sank onto the sofa with a sigh of relief.

It was short-lived. The phone rang and she snatched it

up. No one spoke.

'Dawn? I know it's you. Look, I'm sorry about the baby but she's being well cared for, I promise. Dawn?'

Could she hear breathing or was she imagining it?

'Speak to me, Dawn. I haven't told the police but ...' She broke off. Supposing her calls were being monitored. Could they do that without her permission? And now she had admitted she knew something she had kept from the police. 'Look, I know how you feel, Dawn. At least, I don't, but unless you contact me and we discuss this properly I may have to ...' But no one was listening. Dawn had ended the call.

Had it been Dawn? It could have been Josh. Surely silent calls were not Josh's style, but she was losing judgement, needed someone she could trust. Kath would listen. So would Harry. But the more she confided in them the more they would urge her to go to the police. Harry might take it out of her hands and tell the police himself.

For the first time, she admitted to herself how afraid of Dawn she was. Apart from Rosalie, and even Rosalie could have pushed any such thoughts out of her head, Izzy was the only one who knew what Dawn was capable of, how dangerous she could be if anyone tried to thwart her. *Dearest Miles,*

I'm seething. No, that would be counterproductive, but you wouldn't credit what's happened. I've known Izzy all my life, well since I was eight, and we used to think we were telepathic but of course we could only work out what the other was thinking because we knew each other inside out. Now this. I know you understand that what I did is for the best. Best for everyone. But because I love you I want to explain properly. I told you about my father. Poor fool. Izzy used to ask about him sometimes – she's always been inquisitive – but her guess was as good as mine. Have you noticed how other people's fathers are always nicer to other girls than they are to their own daughters? It was the right decision, the only one, Miles, because the way I was brought up left me quite unfit to be a mother. I don't imagine I was an easy child although Sylvia – that's Izzy's mother – thought butter wouldn't melt in my mouth. Butter in my mouth. What an odd idea. How far back can people really remember? I remember being five. Starting school. Sitting on a chair that was too small and not knowing what to say when I wanted a pee. I've got a stomach ache today. From eating too much fruit. I think that's enough. I haven't told you much, have I, but it's best in small doses.

Love you, love you. Dawn.

P.S. People say love's an illusion. Oh Miles, we know that's not true.

P.P.S. I'm sending Izzy a big heavy hint she can't ignore. She'll come to her senses. Have to, won't she!

5

Why had she felt obliged to lie to Harry, making up a dental appointment? Heaven knows, she worked extra hours most weeks and for no extra pay. On another day, she might have told him she had something she needed to sort out, something personal, but Harry had been in one of his moods, answering the phone and indulging himself in a shouting match with whoever was unfortunate enough to be at the other end of the line. Slamming down the phone and snapping Kath's head off for making a minor and easily remedied error. In any case, she had already decided that confiding in Harry was risky.

Now, on her way to Exmouth, Izzy tried to work out how much she would tell Mrs Bruton. No more than was necessary, but sufficient to persuade her it was worth letting her into the house. That might be easier said than done. When Izzy explained that she was a friend of Dawn Dear's, she was likely to have the door slammed in her face. And there was no way she could mention the baby.

She could pretend she needed to trace Dawn's whereabouts because of some legal matter, but that was hardly likely to lead to many revelations from Mrs Bruton, quite apart from the fact she would dislike deceiving her. Probably best to come straight out with the truth – but without any reference to Cressy – say she was worried about Dawn, and so was Dawn's mother. Say she felt bad about calling round, but tracing Miles seemed to be the only way of finding her.

The sky was overcast, and now the weather had turned warmer, rain threatened. In the summer the road to Exmouth would be jammed with holidaymakers' cars and caravans but today it was relatively free of traffic. As she drove through a village, she caught a glimpse of the estuary, a broad band of water that had little in common with the mud flats up in Cheshire, apart from being a popular spot for bird watchers.

Exmouth had a wonderful sandy beach, and Izzy remembered how she and Josh had walked high up on the cliff. At one point, steeps steps led down to the sand and as they descended, Josh had given her a push then caught hold of her arm. *That wasn't funny, Josh.* He had laughed, pulling the face that meant he thought she was too cautious, ought to enjoy living dangerously. How could she have fallen in love with him? But nothing was that simple. You let yourself be carried away, overlooked the warning signs.

Don't think about it. Concentrate on the job in hand. Eight days had passed since Cressy had been left outside her house. Since then, she had spent hours and hours going over in her mind what could have happened to Dawn. Perhaps the baby's name was pure coincidence. But then the parcel had arrived with the familiar teddy bear, and the demand that she, Izzy, was supposed to be looking after Cressy was so typical of Dawn, who had always fought to get her own way. And, there were the phone calls. Not that she could prove it was Dawn. Who was she fooling? Of course Cressy belonged to Dawn.

Where was she? At first, Izzy had assumed she must have been passing through the area, or come to Exeter specially, then returned to where she was living. But the follow-up letter indicated Dawn had seen the local paper, and the television appeal for the mother to come forward. Supposing the threat was a real one. Dawn might be unwell, having a breakdown, suffering from postnatal depression. But what about Miles? Had he stayed on in Portugal? Surely not when he knew she was pregnant. None of it made sense. Izzy had no right to keep information from the police. But supposing she told Fairbrother and it precipitated a clumsy investigation that led to Dawn taking her own life. Plenty of people made threats. Dawn was the kind that carried them out.

As she drove, Izzy decided she would have to discuss her worries with Kath, tell her every detail and see how she responded. If Kath insisted the police must be informed, she would give herself two more days and then contact Linda Fairbrother. Or would she? Ever since she found Cressy on her doorstep, she had been expecting Kath to give her some moral support, ask how she was feeling, take her out for a drink. But recently the support had failed to materialise. Why? Did Kath think she was behaving irresponsibly? What would she have done in the circumstances? Perhaps it was just that the whole thing reminded Kath of her own start in life, but if that was the case they could have discussed it. Lately, Kath never seemed to want to discuss anything.

The car in front had two grey-haired women in the back and two old men in the front. It was being driven very slowly, which was all the more irritating since the driver in the van behind Izzy was acting as if she was the one who should be getting a move on. Applying her brake, she watched as the van swerved in a skid then pulled out and overtook on a corner. Stupid bastard, but as luck would have it – his luck – nothing was coming the other way. The van was a green one. Dave's van? Dave's van, being driven by Josh?

The car with the four old people had virtually come to a standstill. Izzy glanced at the clock then realised she had reached the outskirts of Exmouth and would have to decide whether to turn into the town centre or drive towards the seafront.

It wasn't a town she knew well, and she had no street map, so she would have to stop and ask for directions. Still, what difference did it make what time she turned up at the house? There was very little likelihood of her being made welcome.

Miles Bruton's house turned out to be in a no-through road. Parking a short distance away, Izzy stood on the opposite pavement and watched the house for several minutes. She had assumed Wendy Bruton lived on her own, but if Dawn had been telling the truth, the marriage could have failed because his wife had been having an affair, in which case her lover might have moved in. No point speculating. She would have to face whatever she found.

The front door opened and two teenage girls came out, both talking so loudly Izzy could hear every word. They were planning to call round at a friend's place and finish an assignment. The friend was good at Maths – what would they do without her – and she didn't mind if they copied her homework. The conversation reminded Izzy of how Dawn had always sailed through Maths, failing to understand how anyone could find it difficult; not that she could be accused of being a swot. She had been popular at school, except for that one incident …

The two girls had disappeared in the direction of the town centre. Who were they? Relatives of Wendy Bruton's, or perhaps they were renting a room. No, they were too young for that, still at school. If this was the right house, what was she going to say? *Excuse me, but are you Mrs Bruton? Only I'm looking for Dawn Dear, the person who went off with your husband.* She would have to work round to the subject, tactfully, cautiously, but how could she? Inventing a covering lie would be even worse and if Wendy Bruton refused to speak to her it would be only what she deserved.

Izzy crossed the road, walked through the open gate, and pressed the bell. The wait before anyone answered was so long that at first she thought everyone must be out then a man appeared, dressed in overalls and holding a screwdriver.

'Yes?' He had the resigned expression of someone who expects to be asked to give money to charity.

'I'm sorry to bother you,' Izzy said, 'but I'm looking for a Mrs Bruton, only I think she may have moved.'

'She has.' The man turned to look back inside the house. 'Someone who wants Wendy Bruton,' he called.

'She didn't leave a forwarding address.' He was joined by a large woman with a shiny red apron. 'Or a phone number. We still get mail for her but I'm afraid I've started throwing it away.'

'So you've no idea where she lives? Or even if she's still in the area?'

'Oh, she's still around,' the woman said, 'she wanted somewhere smaller, but as far as I know she was going to carry on with her job at the hospital. Are you a relative?'

'A friend. I've been abroad. We lost touch. Did something happen?'

The two of them looked at each other but said nothing.

'Not something with Miles?' Izzy sounded genuinely concerned.

'You'll have to ask her,' the woman said, 'as I told you, we don't know her address but the place she moved to was the other side of town, a bungalow I believe, with just enough room for her and the little boy.'

Little boy? Izzy managed to keep her expression unchanged. 'Thanks, anyway. Sorry to take up your time.'

The man opened his mouth to say something then turned to his wife to check her reaction.

'If you find her,' the woman said slowly, 'only Abbi – that's our daughter – she saw her a few days ago.'

'Saw Mrs Bruton?'

The woman nodded. 'Said she was crying. I wouldn't be telling you this but if you're a friend you might be able to help. I felt sorry for her having to sell up. Her husband had left her, gone off with another woman. After we moved in, she came round a few times, once to collect a painting she'd left in the attic, and other times to pick up her mail.'

'You didn't ask for a forwarding address?'

The man shook his head. 'She said the post office would be re-directing. All sounds a bit strange to you I expect, but we took quite a liking to her. And the little lad. Then all of a sudden she stopped calling and we haven't heard from her since – must be the end of April.'

When she checked, Wendy Bruton no longer worked at the local hospital but was employed at a private clinic. Would she be working there today? And even if she was, would she agree to talk? It seemed unlikely.

Since learning that Wendy had a son, Izzy was even more convinced that Dawn had lied about Miles' marriage being over before she met him. If she had been speaking

64

the truth, she would have mentioned the boy without any feeling of guilt. How old was he? Miles was nearly twenty years older than Dawn so presumably his son was in his teens, could even have left home.

The clinic was housed in a single-storey redbrick building with a car park, most of which was marked out for its employees. Izzy had squeezed into the small space permitted for visitors. Now she had to find out if Wendy Bruton worked there full-time and if so when it might be possible to have a word with her.

Behind the desk, in an opulent foyer, a woman sat inspecting her perfectly manicured nails. She was probably in her early fifties but had spent time and money on her appearance, particularly her clothes.

'You have an appointment?' Her eyes remained fixed on her hands.

'No.'

'Who was it you wanted to see?'

'Mrs Bruton. Wendy Bruton.'

The woman looked up. 'She's fully booked, you may have to wait several weeks. Hang on, I'll check.'

'It's personal,' Izzy said, cutting short the receptionist's leisurely flicking through the appointments book, 'is she here now and if so can you tell me when she's likely to be free? It won't take very long. It's quite important.'

The receptionist picked up a phone and pressed a buzzer. 'Wendy, there's someone who wants to see you. She says it's personal. Her name?' The receptionist glanced up, waiting.

'Isabel Lomas. Tell her I'm a friend of Dawn Dear.'

As the information was passed on, Izzy held her breath. Would Wendy Bruton say she was too busy or would her curiosity get the better of her? What would she do in her situation?

'Mrs Bruton will see you now but she only has five minutes before her next client is due.'

Izzy was escorted through a swing door and the receptionist pointed down a long corridor and said Mrs Bruton's room was the last on the right, and there was a nameplate on the door.

Listening to the sound of the woman's heels fading in the distance, Izzy tried to picture what Wendy Bruton would look like. What would she be expecting to hear? Had something happened that Izzy knew nothing about, or would she have more information about Dawn than Wendy Bruton did?

The door opened before Izzy had reached it and a small dark-haired woman came out to meet her. She wasn't pretty but her pointed features gave her a pixie-like appearance and in her own way she was rather attractive.

Izzy held out a hand. 'Thank you for agreeing to see me.'

'What choice did I have?' The door was held open for her to enter and Wendy Bruton sat down behind a desk, making Izzy feel at even more of a disadvantage.

Her consulting room was more homely than Izzy had expected. The walls were covered in modern prints and several good pieces of pottery stood on the window sill, along with an unusual pot plant, the kind that needs plenty of care and attention.

'I need to trace Dawn,' Izzy explained, 'I'm sorry, you must think me very insensitive, but I had no idea who else I could ask.'

'You say you're a friend of hers.'

Izzy nodded. 'We went to school together. I haven't heard from her since February and neither has her mother. She said she was coming back to England but that was the last any of us heard.'

'And why did you think I'd be able to help?'

Izzy struggled to find the right words, although in the circumstances what would be "right"? The woman at her old house had said her daughter had seen her crying. She didn't look the type to cry in the street – she looked in perfect control – but anyone has their breaking point. 'Look, if you've no idea where she is just say so and I won't bother you again.'

Wendy gave her a cold smile. 'I think I have a right to know what all this is about.'

'Yes, of course, but really there's nothing else I can tell you.'

'In that case I can't help.'

Izzy stood up to leave, but there was something about Wendy's expression that made her hesitate. 'Look, I can't prove it but I've reason to believe Dawn may be ill. No, I don't mean physically ill. What I'm saying, I think there's a possibility she might take her own life.'

'I see.' Wendy's tone had not altered. 'What makes you say that?'

'The last letter she wrote to me. Something seemed to be worrying her. I've known her most of my life and I've never heard her so agitated and –'

'I thought you hadn't heard from her for some time.'

'No. I haven't.' Perhaps she should tell her the truth. But how could she? Wendy Bruton would be only too glad to let the police know Dawn had left her baby outside someone's house. Did she know about the baby? Was that why she had been crying?

'I thought her mother would know where she was.' Izzy had decided to try a different tack. 'She lives in Cheshire – her mother I mean – and she hasn't been well. Actually she's very ill.'

'You're talking about Dawn's mother?' Wendy Bruton

67

looked at her watch. 'In that case, I suppose I shall have to tell you what I know. Not now. I have a client then I'll have finished for the day. I'll give you my address and you can join me there in an hour's time. No, make it a little longer in case I'm held up.'

It was months since Izzy had walked on the beach. The tide was out and below her a wide expanse of sand stretched towards the distant sea where a single walker was exercising his dog. As Izzy watched, the terrier leapt in the air, catching a ball in its mouth and lolloping back to its master.

The thought of taking a dog for a walk appealed to her and if she could find a breed that liked cats, and didn't mind being left on its own all day, she might consider having one. Was there such a breed? Dogs were pack animals that needed a leader. Was the same true of human beings? It was something she and Dawn had discussed when they were going through their philosophical phase. Without a clear hierarchy did people feel so anxious they were drawn to anyone strong, powerful? Was that why Dawn had joined the community in Scotland? And if its leader turned out to be shallow and hypocritical, why had it taken her so long to find out?

Walking on sand made Izzy want to take off her shoes. In October? It was reasonably warm but the water would be freezing cold. A proper beach, with cliffs and rock pools, and sand that remained sandy instead of turning into treacherous mud.

The dog approached her, with its nose to the ground, sniffing. Izzy reached out to touch it but it shied away and started racing round in ever-increasing circles.

'Only eight months old,' the dog's owner, an elderly man, explained. He turned to stare up at the cliffs. 'I was here when it happened.'

'I'm sorry.' Izzy had no idea what he was talking about.

'You're not local then? I thought you'd have read about it if you walk here regularly. Young woman on the edge – there's a gap in the hedge – looked like she was going to jump.'

'But she didn't.'

He shook his head. 'Another woman managed to approach her, without being seen. Must have persuaded her. I was holding my breath. I mean, it could have made her jump sooner. Then, all of a sudden, the woman on the edge seemed to change her mind.'

It was fairly close to where Josh had pretended to push her over. 'What happened? I suppose she was taken to hospital. You don't know which one?'

'Ran off.' He had his hand on the dog's collar. 'Didn't even thank the woman who'd saved her life. In trouble I expect. These days, young people don't think about the consequences. Live now, pay later. Get what they deserve.'

Izzy disliked the man's attitude, knew his type, but she needed to find out as much as she could. 'Can you remember what she looked like?'

'Looked like? What are you, a reporter from the local paper?'

6

She had left an hour and ten minutes, just as Wendy Bruton had requested, but when she reached the house she was greeted impatiently.

'I thought you'd changed your mind.' Wendy showed her into an extremely tidy room that smelled of furniture polish, and asked if there was anything she would like to drink, coffee or tea.

'No, thank you. This won't take long. As I said at the clinic, I'm really here on behalf of Dawn's mother. It's unlike Dawn to remain out of touch for so long although I realise –'

Wendy waved aside the explanation with a slight toss of her head. 'I've already decided I'll tell you everything I know. It's in my interest as well as yours. Miles has always been a pathological liar. The only way to outsmart those kind of people is to gather conflicting stories from as many sources as possible then present the person with your evidence.'

'Yes, I see.'

'I don't suppose you do.' Wendy's formal way of speaking was in keeping with the orderliness of her house, but beneath the objective manner she was struggling to keep a grip on herself. 'Sit down then. Anywhere. Wherever you like. Miles wrote to me after they came back from Portugal, to tell me he'd made a terrible mistake and wanted to come home.'

Izzy opened her mouth, but Wendy indicated that if she wanted to hear the whole story she would have to be allowed to tell it without interruption. 'Naturally I wasn't going to let him return, and carry on as if nothing had happened, so I wrote back and more or less told him it wasn't on.' She paused, glancing at Izzy then rubbing the palms of her hand together ending with a small clap. 'I suppose I wanted him to beg. Well wouldn't you?'

It was a rhetorical question but Izzy nodded in agreement. The room, with its immaculate décor, was almost clinical and Izzy suspected Wendy was one of those people who plumped out the cushions as soon as her visitors had left. Did she have any visitors or was her life divided into work all day and caring for her child in the evenings and at weekends?

'Anyway,' Wendy continued, 'by the end of April, Miles had said sufficient for me to suggest he return home and we would give it a trial. So to cut a long story short, he's been living here since the beginning of May and Dawn stayed on in Kent.'

'Kent?' Izzy could keep quiet no longer. 'Whereabouts in Kent? You mean your husband is living here now and – '

Wendy raised her left hand, and Izzy noticed she still wore a wedding ring. 'He was here until the Sunday before last then, following a phone call, he said he was popping out to see a friend. He hasn't been back since.'

'You've reported him missing?'

She shook her head. 'Not much point, is there? Just

adding more humiliation. Obviously, once he'd got me back, in a manner of speaking, he missed Dawn. You know I think his ideal would have been to carry on having an affair with her while he was still living with me. Lots of men would like that, wouldn't you say?'

'So you haven't heard from him since he left?'

'Not a word, and he needn't thinks he can do the same thing over again. I'll tell you one thing though, I've a feeling Dawn may have moved into the area. He'd changed his mobile number, but someone rang the landline and when I answered the call was ended immediately.'

'But what makes you think she's living nearby?'

Wendy bent to pick up a piece of fluff on the carpet. 'The second time it happened I checked and it was a local number.'

'Did you make a note of it?'

'I was going to ring back but ... I wasn't sure ... What could I say? It could have been her who answered and from the brief remarks Miles made about her I ... this may sound pitiable but I was afraid.'

The door had creaked open and a small boy of about six or seven was standing staring at her.

'Dominic, I told you to stay in your bedroom.' Wendy sounded unreasonably harsh, then noticed the boy's expression and reached out to pull him close to her. 'This is my son.'

'Hello.' Izzy smiled at the boy while secretly cursing him for interrupting the conversation just when she was hoping Wendy might have been going to tell her something important. No, how could she curse him when he was so young and looked so worried. Dawn should have told her Miles had a child. Perhaps she felt ashamed that she had taken him away from his son. Not that Dawn was one for feeling shame. In fact, it was one of the emotions she considered to be pointless. *What good does it do, Izzy? Teachers always want you to feel ashamed if you haven't done your best work. What I do is up to me.*

'Go and wait in the kitchen, Dominic,' Wendy told the boy, 'I'll only be a few more minutes.'

He hesitated, rubbing his turned-up nose. He was the image of his father, same round face and sandy hair. He had even inherited Miles' short-sightedness, although the frames of Dominic's glasses were transparent whereas Miles' had been horn-rimmed. His jeans looked newly pressed. So did his grey sweatshirt with a picture of a fox on the front. Izzy pictured immaculate bedrooms, his and Wendy's, with clothes neatly folded or hung, and nothing out of place. His toys would be the same, lined up or put away in boxes. Could you pass on your obsessional behaviour to your child and if you tried would he or she rebel during their teenage years?

'Go on, Dom.' Wendy raised her voice and the little boy's mouth turned down. 'Oh, I'm sorry, darling, but this lady used to know Daddy, she might be able to help us find him.' Then, turning to Izzy. 'I'll give you the number provided you promise to get in touch if you find out where they are. I suppose I could have rung it myself but quite honestly I haven't been able to face speaking to either of them. If it was just me – but there's Dominic to think about. Before all this happened the two of them were inseparable.'

Dominic was standing outside the door. Izzy could see one of his white trainers. She wondered if there was anything he could tell her that might throw light on where Dawn and Miles were living. Children picked up far more than adults realised. It had been the same when she was a child and her parents spoke in French, thinking they wouldn't be understood. If Dawn had been in the house when it happened, the two of them had rushed upstairs and grabbed Izzy's French dictionary. *What's the French for pregnant?* They usually assumed her parents had been talking about some friend or relative who was unmarried and having a baby. Otherwise, why couldn't they speak openly?

Having a baby when you weren't married? How unimportant it seemed in the current circumstances. Dawn would never have seen the lack of a husband or boyfriend as a reason to give away your baby. For a desperate measure like that she must be in serious trouble.

Dominic had crept back in. He approached Izzy, uncurling his fingers to show her a black plastic figure, with a green mask and a laser in its hand.

'That's nice,' she said, 'what's he called?'

'I told you to stay in the kitchen, Dominic.' Wendy sounded close to tears. 'No, it's all right, come and sit down.'

The boy sat on the floor next to Izzy. 'He's got special powers,' he said.

'Yes, I'm sure. What can he do?'

'Kill people,' he muttered fiercely, 'and do magic on them to make them come alive again.'

Wendy interrupted to say she had thought it was going to rain but the sky seemed to be clearing.

The weather, a safe subject to return to, but nothing about Wendy gave the impression she felt safe.

Driving home, Izzy tried to collect her thoughts. It was clear Wendy Bruton knew nothing about a baby. But why should she? Miles would have been unlikely to tell her. Except how did he think he was going to patch up his marriage and give Dawn money for the baby without his wife finding out? Was there a baby? It was the name Cressy that had started everything off, but she and Dawn had thought of other names too.

At one time, Dawn's favourite boy's name had been Howard and her favourite girl's name, Marigold. *If you had a baby and it was a boy* ... Izzy herself had gone through at least half a dozen names. Suzy for a girl. Or, Kirsty, or Eva. For a boy, she had chosen Alistair or Joshua. Joshua? She thought about Josh and gave an involuntary hollow laugh. Little had she known, little did anyone know how their adult life was going to turn out.

Once they had started at the comprehensive they never played the game again. It was too babyish. Still, however hard Izzy tried to convince herself, there was no denying that the last few times they had played it, Dawn had settled on the name Cressida and even started to picture what her daughter would look like. *Cressida, Izzy, don't you think it's the best name ever. Cressida, and Cressy for short.* A coincidence? If it had been just the name ... But there was the parcel, with the bear. That had to prove something.

Dominic was a name Izzy liked but she couldn't recall thinking of it while they were playing their game. They had played other games too. Ones Rosalie would have disapproved of and Izzy's mother might not have too pleased either. Dawn's favourite game was sticking pins in a rag doll she had made herself. One of them chose a victim, sometimes a strict teacher who had punished one of them, or Dawn was more likely to select a member of their class. A girl called Elaine was the most likely, her crime being that she sometimes did better than Dawn in a maths test. The game with the pins had made Izzy uneasy but she was too in awe of Dawn to say anything, although later she would feel guilty. In case the pins worked. Except how could they, and what were they supposed to do? Saying she was 'in awe' of Dawn was re-writing history. In truth she had been afraid of her, not all the time but when Dawn was in full flow, plotting revenge with that grim expression on her face.

Her thoughts returned to Wendy Bruton. So far, Izzy had assumed Dawn had fallen for Miles and forced him to leave his wife. But it might not have been like that. Wendy, with her ultra-tidy house, could have made his life unbearable and he might have been looking for a way out when he met up with Dawn. How had they met? Izzy had an idea they had bumped into one another in a cinema. Dawn had been on her own and so had Miles. But with Dawn, fact and fiction were indivisible. Some of her stories were true. Others were inventions and it seemed to amuse her when Izzy had questioned her to try and discover the truth. How would it be if she found her now? But it was no good worrying about that. Dawn would be incapable of hiding the fact that she had given birth to Cressy.

When she returned to the office, Izzy almost forgot she was supposed to have had a dental appointment. One lie followed another, and she even found herself holding the left hand side of her jaw.

Harry and Kath had been whispering when she opened the office door and she felt certain they had been talking about her. Did Harry know she had made up the toothache? They were watching her, both of them, then Kath gave a brittle laugh and began talking about the project they were working on and how the layout looked all wrong.

'It's what the client wants.' Harry stretched out his legs. 'I made a few suggestions but they were all turned down.'

'I know, Harry,' Kath drawled, 'but if she doesn't like

it she'll blame us. Should I give her a ring and she can have a look at what we've done so far?'

Harry opened a drawer. He seemed not have heard what Kath said. Either that or he had something else on his mind. In any case, Izzy was fairly certain the conversation about the client had been thought up to disguise the fact they had been discussing her state of mind and both of them thought she was losing the plot.

'This baby,' Harry said, 'you don't suppose you were chosen specially, perhaps by someone you've been kind to in the past?'

'How do you mean?' Instantly Izzy was on guard.

'I don't know.' Harry was still looking in his desk drawer. 'A friend of a friend? Friend of Josh's? Just a suggestion.'

He and Kath exchanged glances and Izzy responded angrily. 'If the two of you have been discussing me behind my back I'd prefer to know what you were saying.'

'Whoa.' Harry slammed the drawer shut. 'Don't be like that. We want to help, don't we Kath, but you seem unwilling to let us. And as a matter of fact, we were talking about something entirely different.'

Izzy was starting to feel unwell. Not her teeth, although that would have been a judgement for telling a lie, but her head throbbed and her neck felt stiff. 'If you must know, I've been to Exmouth. To see someone who might know what's going on. She didn't so that's an end to it. And you're starting to sound like DS Fairbrother, Harry.'

She wanted to go home and go to bed. If Josh was there he would have made her a hot drink and sat on the bed, listening to what had happened. Like hell, he would. Josh had never been able to stand it if she was ill. *I'm not good with sick people, Izzy, something to do with my mother.* It had often been something to do with his mother.

Dearest Miles,

Izzy tried to get her back but returned home empty-handed. I expect it will take a few more days. You don't like Josh, do you, but I think he'll make a good father when he comes round to the idea. He's a fool but that means he can easily be manipulated. Lions kill the offspring of females with whom they want to mate. We're all animals, of course, but our superior brains mean we can rise above such base instincts. I know Izzy inside out – she'd be more than a match for any man. No, I'll rephrase that. More than a match for Josh. It's cold today and my back aches from re-arranging stuff so the garage door can be closed properly. Do you think Cressy can smile or will she wait until she's settled into her proper home? The house in Dawlish must be some kind of hostel. I reckon Izzy panicked – it would be typical of her - but it will all work out how we want it to in the end. In my experience, if you want something badly enough you can always get it. We know that, don't we, Miles?

Love you, love you, Dawn

7

She had phoned the number that Wendy Bruton had given her five times and on each occasion it rang but no one answered. After one more unsuccessful attempt to get through, she set off to visit Cressy's foster family. It was after six but traffic was still heavy and it was not until she reached the edge of the city that she started to relax and think about what she was going to say to Bev and Alan Jordan.

Nine days had passed since the baby had been left outside her house. What was it like being a foster parent, particularly when such a young child had been put in your care? How could you fail to become attached to it? And the other children – Nigel and Pippa – how were they going to feel if the real mother turned up?

No doubt Bev had explained to them repeatedly how Cressy was only there for a few weeks. Would it make any difference? Bev had fostered other children on a short-term basis but in each case the child had been much older, and the length of its stay known in advance.

In her driving mirror, she spotted a green van. It was not directly behind her – there was another car in between – so it was impossible to catch a glimpse of the driver. Was it Josh? He drove an ancient Saab but he could have borrowed Dave's van. So he could follow her, check up on her, because he had accused her of getting rid of him so some other bloke could move in? It was something he and Dawn had in common, a determination to get their own way, but there the resemblance ended. There was nothing stupid about Josh, but he lacked Dawn's sharp intelligence, her ability to look ahead, like a chess player – and her ruthlessness.

Did Josh love her? Had he ever loved her? What was love? Sexual attraction, mutual dependency, attachment born out of familiarity?

What was she doing? It was right that absence sometimes made the heart grow fonder, but the expression, "familiarity breeds contempt" also had some truth to it. If she was honest with herself, Josh had taken her for granted, almost as soon as he moved in. Love is blind – another cliché that rings true. She had accepted his excuses: his mother had spoiled him because he was the only boy in the family or – and this was the feeblest excuse of all – his father had expected everything done for him so it must be genetic!

Dawn and then Josh. Did she attract self-centred people? Did she enjoy playing the role of the martyr? No, none of that was true. At her best, Dawn was a good friend, exciting to be with, amusing, loyal. When they resurrected their friendship in Exeter, she had seemed remote, preoccupied, but the fact that she had left her baby outside Izzy's house meant she still trusted her. Cressy was her baby. Izzy was sure of it. Her attempts to convince herself it was "just a baby" always failed. The notes were not Dawn's usual style – she prided herself on her ability to write good English – but she had needed to be anonymous, quite apart from the fact that she must be under severe stress.

When she reached the junction at the edge of the town, the van was still following, but the driver of a slow-moving Citroën had allowed another car to come out of a side road in front of him so it was even harder to see. As well as that, it had started to rain, big drops that splashed on the windscreen then stopped as quickly as they had started so that the wipers dragged and squeaked. Her car needed a service. Wouldn't it be typical if it broke down just now?

Taking the right fork, she thought she saw a flash of green turning left. Josh knew roughly where the foster parents lived –though not their exact address – but why would he have any interest in following her there? She was imagining things; there must be dozens of green vans about, and in any case it could have been Dave on his way to meet some friends.

She ought to be relieved that Josh had taken her words at face value and stayed away. She was relieved, of course she was, but she wanted him to suffer and suspected when he begged her to let him move back in, he had simply needed to prove he could always get what he wanted, that he was irresistible. Was he still living with Dave? What did it matter? Put him out of her mind. Concentrate on Cressy – and Dawn. Cressy ought to be reunited with her mother, but in the state she was in Dawn was unlikely to be able to look after her and she was far better off with Bev Jordan. What about Miles? He had a right to know what had happened to his daughter. Perhaps he did know. Perhaps he and Dawn had planned the whole thing together.

Parking her car in the same place as before, Izzy walked

back to the Jordans' house, trying to ignore the growing sense of unease that she had not told the police about the teddy bear and the accompanying note. Did anyone have the right to control another person by threatening suicide? But Dawn could be severely depressed. Since her conversation with Wendy Bruton, it had become clear that Dawn had been on her own for a time. Although it was possible Miles had lived with Wendy and still visited Dawn.

How had Dawn spent the time? Trying to persuade Miles to come back? And why had he finally agreed? She had lied about him having a child and no doubt there had been other lies too. As far as Izzy could tell, Miles had said very little to Wendy about his time in Portugal and she had decided not to grill him but concentrate on trying to put their relationship back together again. For Dominic's sake, she had implied, although Izzy had the impression she still loved her husband.

After she left Exmouth, Izzy had thought of dozens of questions she could have asked but it was important not to alienate Wendy as she might need to speak to her again. The little boy had been a shock. So young and, if Wendy was telling the truth, so attached to his father. Dawn had never met him but she would have been jealous of him nevertheless. Was he in danger? No, she would never harm a child.

Bev answered the door with Cressy in her arms. 'Come along in, the others have gone to the cinema so you'll be able to see her in peace. Actually I was just about to give her a bath.'

'Fine by me.' Izzy had never bathed a baby in her life but presumably she was only going to be there as a spectator.

Cressy looked larger. It was impossible in such a short

time, but her cheeks looked fatter.

'She can smile,' Bev said. 'Nigel was the first to notice. I worry they're becoming so fond of her, especially Nigel. I caught him bending over her cot kissing her. Did you know, they say kissing evolved from animals giving their young food from their mouths? Do you suppose that's right?

Izzy laughed. 'Sounds a possibility.'

'Not a word about the mother.' Bev was halfway up the stairs with Izzy following her. 'You haven't heard anything? Imagine how the poor soul must be feeling. Doesn't bear thinking about.'

The door to one of the bedrooms was wide open and as they passed Izzy could see a row of soft toys arranged across a pillow. A spotty dog, a giraffe, and a much-loved bear. 'Ever since Cressy was left outside my front door, I've been trying to work out if there could have been a special reason for leaving her there.'

Bev turned round sharply as she entered the bathroom. 'You think that's possible?'

'Not really.' Izzy disliked lying to Bev. She was so open, so lacking in deviousness ... although when she thought about it she hardly knew her at all. 'The police have been round twice and I've a feeling they think I'm keeping something from them.'

'Oh, they're always like that.' Bev had undressed Cressy and was slowly lowering her into the water. The baby gave a little gasp then relaxed, screwing up her nose when her face was wiped with a soft sponge.

Bev turned to look at Izzy. 'Alan and I were turned down for adoption. We'd been trying for a baby of our own for years – I'm older than Alan, not much, but there's a lower age limit for women.'

'Why?' Izzy was outraged.

Bev smiled. 'Social workers are a law unto themselves. No, that's not fair, some of them are all right. After all, it's the children they're concerned for, not their adoptive parents. Cressy had a check-up yesterday. No problems, everything's fine. Yelled her head off when the health visitor put her down on the table but if you could see what it's like at the clinic, all that noise, pandemonium!'

'She's happy with you. If the mother fails to turn up, if she's still … She's a lovely baby.'

'Yes, she is. People think all babies are the same, but it's not right, some are difficult, unresponsive, others cling to you like little monkeys. Whatever else, I think Cressy was well cared for during the first two or three weeks of her life.'

'The clinic think she's about five weeks old?'

'As far as they can tell. I expect it's difficult if you don't know the birth weight. Some babies have blotchy skin for the first few weeks and little rashes. Her skin is perfect. Very light – she'll need plenty of sunscreen one day – but so smooth. Feel.'

Izzy touched Cressy's cheek. 'Have you fostered lots of babies?'

Bev nodded. 'But only while social services decided what to do with them. With Cressy – well, they won't be able to decide anything until they find her mother.'

'You'd like to keep her?' Izzy regretted her words as soon as she had spoken them. 'To tell you the truth, it crossed my mind for a few moments. Not really, but I did wonder if anyone had ever found a baby and kept it, although when you think about it that would lead to all kinds of problems.'

'Certainly would.' Bev lifted Cressy out of the water, wrapped her in a towel, and handed her to Izzy. 'Take her downstairs. I need to sort out some clothes then you can

86

dress her while I heat her bottle. Did you have younger brothers and sisters? You look like you've done this before.'

'I'm the youngest in my family. Two older brothers.' For some reason Izzy was thinking about her ninth birthday, and how her mother had given her a pink sweater she had knitted for her. It was babyish and she had refused to wear it then seen the disappointment in her mother's eyes. How could she have been so thoughtless? But she was only nine.

Later, when Cressy was asleep, Bev showed her a photograph album with pictures of all the children she had fostered. 'We're so lucky having Nigel and Pippa, but you never quite get over the longing for a baby you've looked after since it was tiny.'

They sat in silence and Izzy assumed Bev was thinking the same as she was. If Cressy's mother was never traced would Bev and Alan be allowed to keep or would she be given to a younger couple? Compared with the rest of Izzy's life, the Jordan house was a calm oasis. Was that why she had come here or was it really because she wanted to study Cressy's face again, to look for any sign of a likeness? There was nothing about her that would have made it unlikely Dawn was her mother. She had the same colouring and the same-shaped face. Did she look like Dominic? Izzy had almost forgotten to check for any likeness with Miles. It was no good: Cressy was far too young. In any case, children didn't always look like one parent or the other. Izzy looked like her father, and her brother Dan looked like their mother, but Peter didn't look like either of them. In fact, Dawn had once suggested Izzy's mother must have had an affair and Peter had a different father. 'No, she'd never do that,' Izzy had protested, and Dawn had laughed, patting her on the head.

It's so easy to get you going!

'Unless the mother's found she'll never be free for adoption,' Bev said, 'well, not for the foreseeable future. Still, it's early days yet. Where do you suppose the poor girl's living? Can't be far off so you'd think someone would have worked out who she is.'

'Yes, I suppose so.' Izzy was wondering how Dawn could bear to have given her up. Was she in some kind of trouble? Would she reappear in a week or two and reclaim Cressy? None of it made sense.

Bev had gone to make coffee. She seemed in no hurry for Izzy to leave and Izzy was enjoying Bev's relaxing company. The room had such a soothing atmosphere – three-piece suite, fluffy rug, telly in the corner with a pile of old DVDs beside it on the floor. A Barbie doll had been propped up on one of the chairs. She was wearing a purple lace evening dress and silver shoes, and her long blonde hair was held in place with a plastic tiara.

Something about the room was making Izzy feel sad. As a diversion, she started comparing it with Wendy Bruton's immaculate house in Exmouth. Was the little boy Dominic expected to be as tidy as his mother? Miles must have found living with someone like Dawn, who prided herself on having no interest in her surroundings, quite a shock. But perhaps it was the fact that she was so different from Wendy that had drawn him to her, although Izzy suspected it had been the other way round. Once Dawn decided she wanted something – or in this case some*one* – she usually achieved her aim.

'Stuart Robbins,' Harry said, 'I ran into him last night and was surprised to discover he thought you'd been up north, drumming up trade on my behalf.'

'I told you, I went to see someone I knew as a child. A

friend of the family.'

'Yes, well be that as it may, Stuart asked me to say if you get in touch he thinks it possible he may be able to help.'

'Help? In what way?'

Harry combed his moustache with his fingers. 'I've no idea, Izzy, I'm only the messenger.'

Kath was unwell and, not for the first time, Izzy was tempted to confide in Harry. In the past, when she had overreacted – usually something to do with work – he had been the calm voice of reason. Never patronizing, never mocking, he listened carefully and gave an objective view of the situation. But if she told him about Dawn being the baby's mother she knew what he would say. *Go to the police. You should have told them straight away*. And when she protested that Dawn had threatened to kill herself?

He was watching her, wanting to get on with his work but unwilling to go back to his office if she needed to talk to him about something.

'Oh, by the way,' he said, 'you remember how I told you enough contracts have been coming in to make taking on another member of staff a possibility? Anyway as a kind of celebration in advance we – Janet and I – wondered if you and Kath would like to come to dinner next Tuesday.'

'Thanks.'

'Good. I spoke to Kath earlier, before she started seeing jagged lines. This migraine thing's a bastard. They say stress is a trigger but I wouldn't say Kath's been overworking would you? Well, no more than usual. Maybe something she ate.'

'They say chocolate, cheese, and citrus fruit are bad for migraines.'

'You've had attacks too?'

'Not often. Actually I think I've grown out of them.' It was true, she was thinking. If stress was a factor, it must be.

Harry handed her a slip of paper. 'Stuart's number if you decide to look him up. 'I haven't an idea in hell what's going on, but don't forget if you're ever in any kind of trouble I'd always do what I could to –'

'Thanks, Harry but I'm fine. It was a shock finding the baby but her foster mother's really nice. In fact, I'm hoping if the birth mother fails to turn up, or she's not able to look after a child, Bev will be able to keep her. She's not allowed to adopt. She's too old, although I don't think she is.'

'You seem to have become good friends with her.'

'Yes. Yes, I suppose I have. The baby's lovely.'

'But the police are no nearer to tracing the mother?'

'Don't seem to be.'

'And you can't help so they've decided to leave you in peace.'

'Yes, I hope so.'

'Good. Good. Well, that's a relief. I was worried about you but if you can draw a line under what happened that's fine. All the same, it might be an idea to give Stuart Robbins a ring. He's a quiet type of man but I think you'll like him.'

'Why does he think he can help? Help in what way?'

'I didn't ask. Something to do with that friend of yours up north?' He gave her a quizzical look, but he wasn't the type to beg.

8

Her first response was to ignore Stuart Robbins' invitation. What had Harry told him? Enough to allow Robbins to speculate about a possible link between an abandoned baby and Dawn Dear? Had Harry told him he thought she was getting herself into a tricky situation? Was it possible that Robbins knew something Rosalie had failed to pass on?

Of course, it could be that Harry was matchmaking. He knew she had taken the split with Josh badly. If that was the case, she had no wish to meet this Robbins and someone telling you you're going to like a person always tends to put you off. Like when a friend raves on about a film. You decide to watch it but part of you is thinking: I bet it's not that great.

Finally her curiosity got the better of her, and she rang Robbins' number only to find he seemed to think it a matter of some urgency the two of them meet.

Now she was on her way, on foot, to a pub that was less than ten minutes' walk from her house. Robbins had suggested that particular pub. Perhaps Harry had told him where she lived. Perhaps not. It was nearly nine – he had chosen a time when she would have eaten – so he didn't have to offer to buy her dinner. Why did she feel so hostile towards him, so defensive? Was it something Harry had said, or was it because she had spent a sleepless night thinking about Josh, and was feeling too upset and confused to find any pleasure in having a drink with another man.

When she opened the heavy swing door, the place was virtually empty – just a young couple staring into each other's eyes – so she was fairly sure the solitary man standing by the bar with his hand round an empty glass must be Stuart Robbins.

She spoke his name, and he turned to face her, and when she could see him properly he looked faintly familiar. Had she met him before? He looked a little like someone she had been at art college with, but he was taller and his hair was curlier.

'Good to meet you.' He held out a hand. 'You're dead on time. Most people are late. What are you drinking? I suggest we sit over there by the window. Tell me what you'd like and I'll bring the drinks and a couple of bags of crisps.'

She had no appetite – had eaten virtually nothing all day – but the offer of crisps went some way to making Robbins seem more human and she decided to ignore the remark about most people being late. It was hardly a criticism of her, and in her opinion being on time was important. Dawn had always turned up late, as though she was saying her time was more important than Izzy's.

Watching him, while pretending to be studying the posters on the wall, she tried to work out what age he was, then remembered how Rosalie had said Dawn had been six when he was eleven. That made him about thirty-three, but if anything he looked older. Tiny lines curved down from the corners of his eyes, and from his nose to the edges of his mouth. He was tall, but not as tall as Josh, brown-haired, whereas Josh's hair was almost black, and his face was square with a small dent in his chin. Comparisons were invidious. They were also pointless. She had no interest in Robbins apart from the fact that he had known Dawn as a young child.

'How are you?' He sat down opposite her. 'Harry told me about the baby you found dumped on your doorstep. Must have been quite a surprise.'

'Yes.'

'Have they traced the mother?'

'No.' Then, because she had sounded a little sharp, 'Not yet. The police are looking but she could have left the area, could be anywhere.'

'Wouldn't she want to know what had happened to her baby? I suppose she could be dead, although surely someone would have found the body.'

'What makes you say that?'

'Oh, no reason. Do you have any theories about it?'

How many more questions was he going to ask? 'The mother might be in quite a bad state. People abandon their babies for all kinds of reasons but you'd have to be fairly distraught –'

'Sorry, you probably don't want to talk about it. I imagine Harry could be something of a slave driver. Just the three of you, is it?'

'Yes, but I expect he told you he's thinking of taking on someone else.' The abrupt change of conversation, designed to spare her feelings, had irritated her. Did he really think she was still upset about the baby? Harry had probably described her, making her sound thoroughly neurotic. 'How long have you known Harry?' she asked.

He thought about it, scratching an eyebrow. 'I don't

really know him that well. He's interested in birds, came to a lecture I once gave then took part in a survey of birds on the estuary. What about you?'

'Sorry?'

'Do you like birds?'

'Yes. I don't know very much about them. I thought it was a lecture on Victorian architecture.'

'Oh yes, you're right. Bird life is my job but I have an interest in old buildings. How about you? What do you get up to when you're not working?'

What could she say? And why all this small talk. She wished he would get to the point. 'I don't actually have any hobbies. My cat. I have a cat.'

He smiled. 'I like cats. Apart from when they massacre birds. Is yours a bird hunter?'

'If she is, she never brings them home. The occasional mouse, but I don't mind that.'

'Good.' He drew in breath to indicate the ice-breaking chit chat was over. 'You must be wondering why I suggested we meet up. I gather you've met Francis and I wondered what you thought of him. It was a surprise to everyone when Rosalie took up with him. He's a devout Catholic. You probably know that already.'

'No, no I didn't. How did you know I'd met him?'

'We keep in touch.'

'You and Francis? I didn't realise. You knew him when you lived there, did you?'

Robbins was fiddling with the top of one of the bags of crisps. When he finally tore it open, crisps flew all over the table and they both laughed, breaking the tension. 'My mother knew his. They weren't friends exactly but they shared an interest in gardening, both belonged to some club that organised flower shows.'

'Meeting Francis was quite a surprise,' she said. 'Until

94

I called round at Rosalie's, I had no idea she was living with someone.'

He looked up, frowning. 'So you hadn't been in touch for a while.'

'No.'

'But you've been trying to trace Dawn.' He glanced at her then looked away. 'Tell me I'm wrong, but I always found her a little strange.'

'What makes you say that?'

'Any particular reason you needed to see her?'

'Not really.' Izzy disliked the direction the conversation was taking. 'We were close as children but we grew apart. I suppose I felt guilty I hadn't made more effort to keep in touch.'

The pub was filling up. A group of men who could have been rugby players had assembled by the bar and were jostling each other like schoolboys. Stuart Robbins followed her gaze and raised his eyebrows. 'Behave like leks,' he said.

'What are leks?'

'Sorry. Places where male animals display and compete for the attention of females. Degree in Animal Behaviour. I expect you went to art college, did you?'

'Yes.' She was going to point out that there were only two females in the pub. But what was the point?

'So you drove all that way to talk to Rosalie.' He returned to the subject of Dawn. 'That was good of you. If she's worried about her I'm surprised she hasn't contacted Missing Persons.'

'Dawn's not a child.' She was drinking a pint of shandy. Wished she'd chosen something stronger. 'There must be tens of thousands of people who haven't communicated with their families for over a year.'

'As long as that?' He lifted his glass then replaced it on

the table. 'So maybe there's some other reason people are getting worried. Francis seems to think she could be in a psychiatric hospital suffering from depression. Apparently after she left the community in Scotland she was in a pretty bad way.'

'Yes, I expect she was, but that was three years ago. What did Francis say exactly? Did he write you a letter?'

'Email. I doubt if Rosalie can use a computer but Francis has always been keen on the latest technology.'

'Emails are the latest technology?'

'No, of course not.' His voice had an edge and she wished she had kept her mouth shut. 'I daresay by now he's abandoned his laptop and has a tablet. It was more the words he used. *Frantic with worry*. He was referring to Rosalie obviously. *Having nightmares about it.* For my part, it triggered off memories of Dawn as a child. She left the area when I was thirteen or fourteen, old enough to remember what an odd little girl she was, only you know her far better than I ever did.'

Izzy was recalling various events in her childhood. The time Dawn had been off school for nearly a month with stomach pains. The incident in the playground when a boy had called her names and she had hit him so he had fallen against a wall and had to have stitches in his head. Still, most people's childhoods contain events they would prefer to forget.

'She was very clever,' Izzy told him. 'I mean, she is very clever. I suppose any eccentricities she might have had were put down to her being gifted, not that she accepted the label. My father thought she ought to go to special classes but Dawn sneered at the idea, said there wasn't any point.'

'As I said, she was always a little unusual.'

'Unusual in what way?'

96

He shrugged. 'Hard to say. One thing. I remember my mother remarking on it. She had a way of smiling when someone else would have kept a straight face, and frowning when you or I might have smiled. Does that make sense? Probably not.'

'Actually it does.' There was so much she had forgotten about Dawn. In the way that people do, she remembered the good parts and her thoughts skated over the bad ones. But had they been so bad?

There was the time she had stolen Izzy's watch – a present from her parents – and hidden it in the drawer where she kept her underclothes. Izzy had searched and searched but it had never occurred to her that Dawn could have taken it. Then one day, when they were in Dawn's bedroom, she had asked Izzy if she wanted to see her new knickers. *Why would I want to do that,* Izzy had laughed. *Go on, go on, have a look.* And there was her precious watch. What had she done? She should have been very angry, told Dawn what she thought of her. Had she been too afraid?

Unpredictable people could be fun to spend time with, but Dawn sometimes carried it too far. She could switch from treating Izzy as her special friend – whispering and confiding – to insulting her, telling her she was stupid. Why had she put up with it? But when you look back on your childhood, Izzy thought, heaps of things are inexplicable.

Stuart had finished his drink, and she expected him to make an excuse and leave, but he seemed in no hurry. 'My mother warned me against her.'

'Against Dawn?'

He drained his glass, glanced at the bar then obviously decided against a refill. 'Girls are more cunning than boys.'

'Are they?'

'Come on, you know they are. Dawn collected insects.' A few broken crisps remained. He gestured to her to eat them and when she declined, picked up a handful and transferred them to his mouth. 'Dead ones.'

'She'd killed them?'

He shrugged again. 'I'm sorry, she was your friend.'

'*Is* my friend.'

'You think she's still alive?'

'Yes, of course, why wouldn't she be?' The conversation was going from bad to worse, but it was her fault for keeping him in the dark about what had been going on.

A second group of young men had come into the pub and she recognised a friend of Josh's, whose name she had forgotten. He spotted her and waved and she waved back, wondering how much Josh had told him. Not that she cared, although she was becoming painfully aware how her investigations were keeping her mind off what had happened between her and Josh. However badly someone has treated you, it's impossible not to feel the loss of a close attachment.

With a jolt, she became aware that Stuart Robbins was holding his empty glass, while watching her closely. 'So you've no idea where she might be? I suppose I'm here on Francis's behalf. He used to do work for my father, in the house and also at the school where my father was headmaster. At the time he was living with his mother. No one ever imagined he would marry but when she died ...'

'Go on.'

'I was thinking what a shock it must have been.'

'For Dawn.'

He smiled. 'Actually I was thinking of Francis. You've lived with your mother for over forty years and suddenly you're alone in the world.'

'You're saying he sees Rosalie as a replacement for his mother.'

'I've no idea. Does it matter? Provided they're happy with the arrangement.' He glanced at the clock on the wall above the bar. 'I can't stay long. Sorry if I've dragged you out for nothing but I suppose I thought I owed it to Francis to do what I could. He's worried about Rosalie, wants to help if he can, probably resents the fact she's so absorbed, thinking about her daughter, he's not getting the attention he deserves.'

Izzy was annoyed. He *had* dragged her out, and for very little reason that she could see. Harry had said meeting up with him might help. Help who?

When they parted outside the pub, no mention was made of another meeting. She walked away in one direction, Robbins in another, and if he'd looked back she would have sensed it. Had Harry given him her phone number? She had his but was unlikely to contact him again.

Her thoughts returned to Josh and whether he would come round to apologise or if he had decided it was best to stay well clear of her.

Back home, she went to bed early and lay propped up, half watching an old film, half thinking about what Stuart Robbins had said. Dawn *was* an unusual person but the way he described her had made her sound almost evil or, at the very least, psychiatrically ill.

Blanche had come upstairs and was kneading the duvet. Izzy put out a hand to stroke her then stopped when she heard noises coming from the next-door house. Or were they out in the street? When the baby cried she had thought at first it was a cat, but that had been the middle of the night. Now it was not yet midnight.

The noises came again and were definitely from next door. Please not squatters. It would mean months of trying to evict them. The police, bailiffs ... And they wouldn't care what kind of state the house got into. Or was she being unfair? They could be homeless people, desperate for somewhere to stay.

Of course, it was possible the previous owners had come back for some reason. Izzy had known them enough to pass the time of day with and they had a school-age daughter called Jade. Since the house hadn't sold, they had a perfect right to be there, but twenty-five past eleven at night seemed an odd time to have called round. The sounds continued for ten minutes or so then she heard a door being locked, followed by footsteps on the pathway outside, and whispering. It was too cold to get out of bed. Besides she had enough on her mind without worrying about what had been going on next door.

Unless it was Dawn. With Miles. But how could it be? She put one foot on the floor, disturbing Blanche who was curled up next to her pillow. Supposing the two of them were walking down the road ...

Hurrying to the window she stared out, trying to accustom her eyes to the dark. Nothing.

9

From an upstairs window, Izzy saw a car pull up in Palmerstone Road and a woman climb out and open the passenger door to let out a small boy dressed in a pale blue tracksuit. It took Izzy a moment to grasp who they were, then she recognised Wendy Bruton's hair and the pointed features of her face. The boy, Dominic, had his back turned but she could see he was still clutching the plastic figure that could 'kill people and do magic to make them come alive again'.

They were coming to see her, or to spy on her, although that seemed unlikely since Wendy had brought her son along. Could she have found out about the baby? Izzy's name had been withheld from the media, as had her address. Plenty of people knew about it – Josh would have told all his friends – but surely none of them had any connection with Wendy.

Neither Wendy nor Dominic was wearing a coat, but they had come by car and would return home without going anywhere else. The forecast had been for heavy rain but it was warm for the time of year.

Downstairs, she waited for the ring on the bell and tried

to prepare herself. Either Wendy wanted more information or she had something to tell her.

Had she brought Dominic for moral support or because she had nobody to leave him with? When he climbed out of the car, it had been impossible to see his expression but from the way he stood on the pavement, waiting for his mother to lock up, Izzy had gained the impression this was not the way he would have chosen to spend his evening.

The two heads passed the house then she heard Wendy's voice asking Dominic if he thought it was the right place. Wendy must have looked it up in the phone book and perhaps she had been expecting something quite different, somewhere smarter, more modern. By the look of it, Wendy's bungalow had built seven or eight years ago.

Impatient to know what they wanted, Izzy pulled open the front door and spoke her name, and Wendy turned round slowly, without smiling, and guided Dominic into the house ahead of her.

'You weren't in the middle of anything?' She made it sound like a social call.

'No, that's fine. It's nice to see you.'

What a stupid thing to say, but in a way it was true. Wendy was not the easiest person to talk to but Izzy had taken a liking to Dominic. And she sympathised with Wendy who might behave the way she did because she was so unhappy.

'I could have phoned,' Wendy was saying, 'but I thought it best you heard it from Dominic in his own words.'

'Yes, good idea.' Izzy was eager to hear what he had to say but she wasn't going to put pressure on him. She offered a range of drinks but Wendy turned them down, without reference to her son.

'We won't stay longer than necessary. I'm sure you value your free time.' She paused, looking round and her next words surprised Izzy. 'I like your house. I sometimes wish I lived in Exeter but with my job I'm better off where I am, although being in a large city can be a comfort. The anonymity I suppose.'

The previous time they met, Wendy had started off talking very formally. This time she seemed a little more relaxed.

Dominic had found Blanche and taken refuge with her, sitting on the floor by the French window that led out to the patio yard. In spite of the warmth in the house, he looked cold, pinched, and pale. 'Are you sure you wouldn't like a drink, Dominic?' Izzy asked, 'I could make you a hot chocolate.'

The little boy glanced at his mother but she shook her head.

'No, thank you,' he said, 'I'm all right as I am.'

All right as I am. He was picking up his mother's way of speaking. Izzy wondered what kind of a father Miles had been. The one time she met him she had found him serious and without much sense of humour, but he had been with Dawn. When he was with his son he could have been quite different. They could have played on the beach together, kicked a football about, built sandcastles, collected shells. There was no doubt Dominic missed him.

Wendy was sitting on the edge of the sofa. She leaned forward and cleared her throat. 'After you left,' she began, stopping abruptly when she was overcome by a fit of coughing. 'It's all right, I'm not infectious. A nervous habit. So silly.'

Izzy wanted to say something that would put her at her ease but could think of no suitable remark. Wendy's navy blue trousers and white zip-up jacket looked almost like a uniform, and she had probably visited her hairdresser that morning although Izzy suspected she rose every day to wash and blow-dry her hair. Everything about her – and Dominic too – was neat and tidy. Dominic's trainers were gleaming white, without a trace of a scuff, and Wendy's own shoes were equally spotless.

'After last time.' Wendy had found a cough sweet in her bag and was sucking it hard. 'I had a talk with Dominic – about the day his father went out and failed to return – and the two of us tried to think if there was anything we could remember, anything that might have given us a clue as to what was going to happen.'

Izzy looked at Dominic but he had his back turned, still stroking Blanche. At his age – six or seven she guessed – how could he possibly be expected to know?

'Mind she doesn't scratch you,' Izzy warned, but he took not notice.

'He's good with animals.' Wendy gazed at her son with pride. 'When he's grown up he wants to be a vet, don't you, Dom? He'll have to work hard, it's a very competitive profession. If I had the money I'd send him to a private school, mainly because the discipline's so much better.'

'And the classes are smaller.' Izzy tried to contain her impatience. 'To get back to what's happened, you must have gone over and over everything in your mind. I know I would have.'

Wendy found a second throat sweet. 'You haven't heard from Dawn? I suppose I hoped you might.'

'I promised to get in touch with you if there was any news.'

'But your first loyalty would be to your friend.'

'Actually, I'm not sure that it would.'

Wendy looked sceptical. 'Come here, Dominic,' she

ordered and the boy sprang to his feet like a soldier on parade then sat down again and gave Blanche an almost defiant stroke, before slowly joining his mother on the sofa.

With one hand on his head, Wendy adopted as calm a tone as she could manage. 'No hurry, darling, just cast your mind back to that day and tell us what you heard Daddy say.'

'When?' Dom had taken off his glasses. He licked a finger and rubbed one of the lenses, and Wendy exploded.

'Dominic, for pity's sake. This is important. Don't you understand? Don't you want to find your father?'

The little boy took a deep breath. 'He was on his mobile,' he said, speaking so faintly Izzy had to strain to hear him. 'Someone telephoned when Mum was in the garden.'

Wendy had got a grip of herself, but was breathing hard. 'Go on, Dom, then what happened?'

'It was hard to hear. I was in the kitchen. I heard Dad say ... He said ... He said whoever it was shouldn't have done it.'

Izzy moved to a closer chair. 'He meant they shouldn't have phoned?'

'I don't know.' Dominic blushed as though he felt responsible for his father's behaviour.

'Did you hear anything else?'

'He said some more I can't remember.'

'Anything, Dominic.' Wendy's hands were shaking. She clasped them together then unclasped them again and began twisting her ring round and round. 'Absolutely anything, no matter how unimportant it seemed at the time.'

Dominic was sucking his fingers. 'He asked if it was the same side as the railway.'

'Railway?' Izzy repeated. 'Are you sure that's what he said?' This was the first definite piece of information about Dawn's whereabouts. If the call had been from Dawn that was. The same side as the railway? Was there a local railway line and if so where did it run? The most likely explanation was that Miles had misheard, but later she would search online for a map of the railway lines, and the ones that had once run through Devon before all the cuts were made.

Dominic was looking through the window, hoping his part in things was over, but Wendy turned towards him, pressing him to continue. 'Can you remember anything else?'

'There wasn't any more.' His voice had become a sleepy defensive drawl. 'I think he might have said the first on the right.'

'Where Dominic?' Izzy asked. 'By the railway? Try to remember.'

The boy's hands covered his face and she wished she had not sounded so impatient. 'I'm sorry.' She gave him an encouraging smile. 'You've done really well remembering so much. Would you like a biscuit? I think I've got some chocolate ones.'

'No, he's all right,' Wendy said.

'Well, I'll fetch some anyway. Won't be a moment.'

Dominic's face brightened. 'What's he called?'

'My cat? Blanche. She's a girl cat.'

When she returned with the biscuits, Wendy was whispering something to her son and Dominic was nodding.

Izzy put the plate down next to him. 'Have a biscuit. Have two.'

Dominic took a biscuit and bit off a small corner. 'I think my dad was checking if he'd heard properly,' he said. 'Then the person said a lot of stuff only I couldn't hear any of it. Then Dad said he'd be there in about thirty minutes depending on the traffic going to the moor.'

'You never told me that.' Wendy took hold of him by his shoulders. 'If you were listening in on the extension I won't be cross. I know I've told you not to but this is far too important to worry about something like that.'

'I told you, it was Dad's mobile. I only just remembered the last bit. If I'd heard more would we know where he is and what's happened to him?'

'Nothing's happened to him,' Wendy said gently. 'We just want to find out where he is, then you'll be able to see him.'

Dominic stood up. 'Is the toilet upstairs?'

'First door you come to,' Izzy told him. 'I'm sorry.' She turned to Wendy. 'This is awful for you, and for Dominic, but at least there's a chance now we may be able to find them. There isn't a railway across the moor, is there?'

'No, no I'm sure there isn't. So you think they're together. Yes, I knew that was what you were thinking.' Wendy had started to cry. 'At one time Miles mentioned something about needing space. People say that, don't they, as an excuse, but since he didn't come back I suppose I've been hoping if he had a little time on his own he might ...'

'I don't know anything, Wendy, but it seems likely he's with Dawn. Unless you can think of someone else who might have phoned your husband.'

'Someone else?' Wendy took a tissue from her handbag. 'You mean another woman.'

'No, I didn't mean that.'

'Life's so unfair.'

'Yes I know. Yes, it is.'

107

'We had a daughter, me and Miles. If she'd lived she'd be three years old the week after next. She was born eleven weeks premature. She had breathing problems.'

'I'm so sorry.' Izzy thought about Cressy, feeding well, putting on weight, giving Nigel her first smile. 'It must take years to get over something like that.'

'Oh, you never get over it.' Wendy had dried her tears and was looking quite fierce. 'I'm only telling you because I think it was the reason Miles left me. He wouldn't talk about it, just bottled everything up. You'd think we could have comforted each other, wouldn't you, but they say it's hardly ever like that. Each person accuses the other of not caring enough.'

'Yes, I can see that might happen.' Izzy was torn between sympathy, and relief that Wendy trusted her enough to confide in her. Although, desperation often brings people closer.

'Once I was playing with Dominic,' Wendy continued, 'and we were laughing, and later Miles said it meant I didn't care if I'd been able to push Nadia's death out of my head, but I was only thinking of poor Dominic and what a terrible time he'd been having.'

Dominic was coming down the stairs. What must it have been like for him when his sister died? Especially if his parents were unable to talk to each other. Standing at the top, he must have overheard the last part of what Wendy had been saying, but Izzy expected him to pretend he had heard nothing and was shocked when she saw his face.

'Dad thought it was his fault,' he said angrily, 'you caught 'flu off him. That's why the baby was born too early.'

'Oh, Dominic.' Wendy rushed to him and gave him a hug. 'I'm so sorry, so sorry.' She turned to Izzy. 'This is dreadful, I never meant to involve you. Is there anything I can do? I'd help you to look for them but how can I? Imagine if we found them.'

'It's all right.' Izzy let them out through the front door. 'I don't know if what Dominic overheard is going to lead to anything but if it does you'll be the first to know.'

'Will Dad come back?' Dominic's voice was a whisper.

'Yes.' How could she promise such a thing, but the little boy looked so desperate. 'I'm sure he will.'

'I did hear one more thing.'

'Yes, yes.' Wendy took hold of him in case he started walking away.

'He said God something. Godforsaken. Is it the name of a place?'

'No, it's just something people say.'

'Godforsaken place,' Dominic whispered, 'he said Godforsaken place. Back of ...'

'Yes.' Wendy hugged and kissed him. 'Clever boy, I knew more of the call would come back to you. "The back of ..." Go on, Dom, go on.'

'It didn't make sense.'

'Never mind.'

'The back of beyond. He said the back of beyond. And something about a stag. No, a deer.'

After they left, Izzy scribbled down notes, trying to remember Dominic's exact words. *The same side as the railway. A turning on the right. A Godforsaken place. The back of beyond.*

So they weren't in the city. At least that much had been established. The stag, corrected by Dominic to 'deer', must be her name, Dawn *Dear,* although why would Miles have repeated something like that? It made no sense.

Izzy found a map and drew a circle round the area Miles would cover if he had left Exmouth and driven for thirty minutes. Obviously the coastline reduced it but it was too large to be much use. No, Dominic had said "in the direction of the moor". Still too vague, but better than searching indiscriminately. It must be near an old railway line, or perhaps the actual line had gone and people walked or cycled where the rails had once been.

Dominic might have got it wrong, or even made things up to keep his mother happy, but it was the only lead she had. It was getting dark. No use going out now, but tomorrow she would make some excuse and spend the afternoon searching. In the meantime, she would think hard if the snatches of conversation Dominic had remembered triggered off anything Dawn had said, any places she had mentioned.

10

Harry was out of the office all day. Izzy worked flat out for most of the morning then told Kath her head was throbbing and she was going home.

'Good idea.' Kath gave her a sympathetic smile. 'Plenty of hot drinks and painkillers. Not like you to be so sensible.'

'If Harry comes back, tell him I've got a temperature.'

'OK.' Kath looked at her curiously. 'But I doubt if he will. Think you'll be all right for tomorrow evening? If not I'd better let him know.'

'Tomorrow evening?' Then Izzy remembered the dinner party at Harry and Janet's. 'Actually that's partly the reason I thought I'd go home early today.'

Kath had her eyes fixed on her computer. 'It's all right, you don't need to explain. Something's happened, hasn't it, something to do with Dawn. I do wish you'd tell me. I could help.'

'I'll explain later,' Izzy promised, 'not that there is much. Just a faint possibility that will almost certainly turn out to be a wild goose chase.'

'You wouldn't like me to come along? I'm quite

interested in geese.'

'Nothing I'd like better, Kath, but someone has to stay in the office.'

'So there aren't going to be any hot drinks and sitting in front of the telly.'

Izzy smiled. 'Later. This trip I have to make shouldn't take long, then I'll go straight home and concentrate on getting well for tomorrow. It's not a bad cold, I can tell. How could it be after all that vitamin C you keep forcing down me?'

'Izzy?'

'What?'

'You're not in any danger?'

'No, of course not. Why would I be?'

'I've no idea but you're not normally so secretive.'

'You've been fairly secretive yourself during these last few weeks.' It was true. Not something Izzy had given much thought to, but Kath had not been her usual self. She was quieter, more controlled. 'I'm sorry, Kath, I've been so self-absorbed I've forgotten to ask if something's going on –'

'Nothing's going on, Iz. I only wish it was.'

The sun came out briefly only to be covered by clouds a few minutes later. It was one of those days when you haven't a clue what the weather's going to do next and you're not sure what to wear. Izzy could have done with a new winter coat but she was putting off buying one, just like she was putting off everything else, the dripping tap in her bathroom, the cracked tiles on her roof that needed replacing, the car service. *When I find Dawn ... When I know for certain that Cressy is her baby ...*

It was all in the mind, it must be, but her mouth really did feel dry and she thought she had the beginnings of a sore throat. The chances of finding Dawn were minimal, so much so that she had given very little thought to what she would do if she did find her. Or rather, what she would say. *I was worried about you, Dawn. No, I'm not checking up on you, I just wanted to make sure you were all right. How did I trace you?* That part would be tricky, best to play it by ear.

As far as the search went, the first thing she planned to do was call in at village post offices and shops – if there were any left – and ask if anyone had seen someone answering Dawn's description. The whole area – the one she had decided to investigate – was a maze of lanes, with small villages dotted about, some of them so small they could hardly be called villages, just a farm and four or five houses.

At the first few shops she drew a blank. No one had seen a woman answering Dawn's description and the people she asked insisted they would have noticed a newcomer to the district. Eventually, after several fruitless attempts – she almost missed the shop, it was so small – the woman behind the counter paused when she told her the description, deferring to another woman who was busy filling shelves. 'Long fair hair? Pretty girl if she'd tidied herself up a bit.'

'Came in once or twice to buy some things for her friend who'd just had a baby,' the second woman said. 'You know, the usual stuff, disposable nappies, and wet wipes.'

'You don't know where she's living? When was this? A couple of weeks ago?'

The woman shook her head. 'I couldn't say. To tell the truth, I thought she might be one of those travellers.'

'But she was on her own? She didn't have a baby with her?'

'Could have been in the car,' the first woman said.

'Oh, she had a car. Did you see what colour it was?'

'Didn't see it, love, but she couldn't have walked here, could she, not unless she was camping out and who'd do that in this weather. Might've been on a bike, I suppose.'

It's quite important,' Izzy urged, 'she could be unwell.'

The women said nothing, but an old man, rooting about in a box of apples, muttered something about the cottage down the lane past the pigs.

'Which lane would that be?'

The old man picked up an apple and gave her a hostile stare. 'From the benefits office, are you?'

'No, no, nothing like that. I'm a friend. We lost touch but I think she may have rented a cottage in this area.'

'That's what they all say.'

A woman, with two small children, had come into the shop and was staring at her. 'And if you could tell me how to reach the lane with the pigs,' Izzy said. 'Just in case she's there.'

The woman behind the counter puffed out her cheeks as though Izzy had asked the way to John O'Groats. 'Keep on half a mile or so till you reach the farm, then the first on the left. Not a farm exactly, more of a smallholding. Got a sign up, 'eggs for sale', you can't miss it. After that, you keep going till you cross a bridge. That's right isn't it, Alf?' She turned to the old man who gave a brief nod. 'And you'll see the pig farm soon after that.'

Izzy followed the instructions carefully but with a mildly paranoid feeling that they might not be correct. Were all villagers suspicious of strangers? Surely not in this day and age when people had second homes and tourists stopped to buy postcards and ice cream, although this particular spot wasn't really a tourist area. It had started to rain, heavy rain that made visibility difficult.

She had forgotten to bring an umbrella. She was going to get soaked. No, there was one in the boot, an old one with two broken spokes, but it would have to do.

Keep going for half a mile then first on the left after the farm. She almost missed the 'Eggs for Sale' notice, probably would have done except she had to slam on her brakes when a pheasant strolled across the road. First on the left. Carry on to the bridge, which she had reached almost at once. Cross over – and there it was.

There was no sign of any pigs but she thought she might be able to smell them and, through a high hedge, she caught a glimpse of what could be their houses, cylindrical metal shelters spaced at intervals in the mud. The rain had stopped as quickly as it had started and, leaving the car on some rough grass, she continued on foot, scanning the surrounding fields for a cottage. Was it even the right lane? Her ears ached and she really did feel she might have a temperature.

A building came into view and turned out to be a dilapidated barn, but round the next corner she caught sight of a house less than a hundred yards on. Hardly picturesque, with its ugly tiled roof and pebbledash walls, but it still fell into the category of cottage, if only because of the straggling plant that covered most of the porch.

There was no doorbell or knocker, but sounds were coming from round the back and after a minute or so a woman appeared, dragging a basket of logs. She was very old, with a lined face and straggly grey hair, and she was breathing hard as though the weight of the logs was too much for her. When she saw Izzy, she paused for a moment then let go of the basket and approached with a friendly smile. 'Looking for something, dear?'

'Yes, yes I am.' There was just a chance the woman might have seen Dawn. 'The lady in the local shop thought there might be someone living down this lane – someone with a baby.'

'A baby?' The woman looked as if Izzy had said a chimpanzee. 'If there is, I've never seen it.'

'Actually, she might be with a man. And the baby might not be there any more. I mean, she could have left the baby with – with her mother.'

'Only one more cottage before the crossroads and that belongs to Mr and Mrs Piggott. Lived there all their lives, they have. No kiddies.'

'Oh, yes I see, I think it must be the wrong lane. Sorry to bother you.'

'You could ask Freda Piggott.' The woman seemed reluctant to let Izzy go. 'She knows about all the comings and goings round here. Trouble is, they're staying with their daughter till the end of the week. Lives in somewhere called Crouch End. Do you know it?'

'It's in London,' Izzy told her, 'so you think they'll be back by the weekend?'

'That's what they said.' The woman's nose had started to run. She wiped it with the sleeve of her coat then, sensing that Izzy was keen to get away, returned to the basket of logs. 'What's her name – your friend?' she called.

'Dawn. Dawn Dear – or if she's using her married name it could be Bruton.' Even as Izzy spoke she decided telling the woman Dawn's name was a mistake. And adding a second name, Bruton, certainly was.

'Dear's a funny name.' It was clear the woman had heard nothing that would be any use. 'And you say you're a friend.'

Izzy nodded. 'Anyway, thanks again and if I don't have any luck I'll call in on Mr and Mrs Piggott when they're back from London.' Would she? Izzy doubted it. In fact, she was beginning to think the whole venture was insane. For all she knew, Dawn was miles away.

Back at the car, she saw it was splashed all over with the mud she had picked up driving through the lanes. It was a waste of time. Under pressure from his mother, Dominic could well have made up what he heard. She felt sorry for the boy, but also annoyed if he had sent her on a pointless search. But his description of the phone call was all she had and it was too soon to give up. Perhaps she should return to the shop where the women had been prepared to help, but perhaps not. It was unlikely they knew any more and, like the old man, would start to suspect she was from the benefits office or a social worker and, in their terms, up to no good.

The sky was overcast but every so often it cleared, changing the passing fields from dark, gloomy places to bright sunlit invitations to a pleasant afternoon walk. As she drove, Izzy watched out for signposts and memorised names, trying to make a mental map of the area but with no expectation she would make any further progress. Quite soon, it would start raining again and she should have had the sense to wear a raincoat.

She passed a pub and remembered how Josh liked them to drive into the country for a meal, and when they did he drank heavily but expected her to stick to orange juice so she was fit to drive them back home. A mile farther on she noticed pigs in a field and wondered if it was worth walking down the adjoining lane, then realised she must be at least three miles from the village shop and it was unlikely she could have misunderstood the directions to that extent.

Something was nagging away in her head but it was not until she reached the main road that it struck her how stupid she had been. The pub. The sign could have done with re-painting but something about it had registered in her brain and Dominic Bruton's voice was clear in her head, a mixture of sadness and anger as he described the phone call he had overheard, his father talking to someone who could have been Dawn. *'The side of the railway.'*

It was only a chance, but she had to be certain. At the first right turning, she made a U-turn and began retracing her route until she turned a sharp corner and there it was. The Railway Inn.

Should she go into the pub and make some inquiries? It looked closed but there might be someone about round the back. She might call in there later but just now it would be best to look for a cottage.

When pressed, Dominic had said a little more. *The first on the right.* Coming from which direction? She drove on, slowing down at the first turning on the right but deciding it would be unwise to drive up in the car. The lane had grass growing in the centre and looked as if it was only used by the occasional tractor. Where did it lead to – there was no signpost – but neither was there any indication it was not a through road. There could be a cottage somewhere along the way, but it was a long shot. Dominic could have forgotten the next instructions – or failed to repeat them. First on the right, Dawn could have told Miles, then continue on up the hill until you come to a small wood ...

Pulling into a gateway, she sat for several minutes, trying to decide what to do next. On the opposite side of the road she could see a gate. If she climbed it, she would she have a slightly better view of the surrounding fields. Would Dawn have chosen such a remote place? Perhaps she had no choice. In any case, Izzy had long since given up thinking she could read Dawn's mind. The Dawn she knew would never have rented a house in the country. But did she really know Dawn at all?

Balanced on the gate, she stared into the distance, grateful at least that the rain had stopped. She thought she could see a house but it was only the sun catching the metal roof of a barn. Then she spotted it. A grey cottage at the far end of a field, surrounded on two sides by tall, leafless trees.

Leaving the car, aware she could incur the wrath of a farmer if she had blocked his way, she set off, keeping close to the edge of the field. The grass was soaking wet and the air felt humid. If she found Dawn ... But there was no point working out what she would say or do. Just now, all she could hope was that she was right about The Railway Inn.

At first sight it had looked impossible to drive up to the cottage but there could be another way to reach it. There was no one about and no distant hum of traffic that might have indicated she was closer to civilization than she realised, just a faint tapping noise that could be a green woodpecker but could be man-made.

Supposing whoever lived in the cottage was watching her making her way up the side of the field. When she saw a gap in the hedge, where the dead undergrowth had been stamped down, she made a quick decision to circle round and approach the cottage from behind. It was madness. How could Dawn be living there? But Dominic's description was all she had.

For a brief moment, she thought she saw a light on in one of the downstairs rooms but it was only the reflection of the setting sun. The windows had curtains, upstairs and down, but the general look was of somewhere deserted, perhaps unfit for human habitation. She was within fifty yards of the place, but no dog had run out to meet her. Everything was silent.

When she reached a side door, it looked like it was the entrance, or at least the way the owner got into the house. Pausing for a moment, she scanned the building for any sign of life, afraid someone might have seen her but almost more afraid no one had been near the place for months, even years. In spite of the sun, she felt chilled to the bone, and turned up her collar, pushing her damp hair out of her eyes.

What next? She could go up the door and bang on it, or she could look around for anything that suggested someone was living there: a dustbin brimming with rubbish, a clean milk bottle, a newspaper with a recent date. The curtains were drawn back, but that was hardly surprising since it was still light. Izzy's mother had always closed the curtains at the first opportunity. *Let's make ourselves cosy.* Did her mother know something about Dawn that she had kept secret? Surely, when Izzy phoned her in New Zealand, her mother would have told her – although she had deliberately sounded unconcerned, as though visiting Rosalie had only just occurred to her.

And what about Rosalie herself? Did she know only too well what Dawn was up to but had been unwilling to tell her? Or for Francis to find out?

In the woods that came up almost to the back door, something, possibly a fox, let out a harsh yelp. Izzy had been edging towards a downstairs window but the sound made her jump back, losing her footing so she crashed against a pile of old roof tiles. Steadying herself on a rickety piece of trellis, she listened – for a door opening, a footstep. Nothing. Staring up at the roof, she could see it was in a reasonably good state of repair, but appearances were often deceptive; the inside might be a tip.

The rain had made the ground slippery, turning an empty flowerbed into mud. If there was anyone living there, by now they were almost bound to have heard her. Surely they would have come out, but perhaps it was a recluse. Someone could be standing, shotgun in hand, waiting for her to make what could be interpreted as a threatening move. Summoning all her courage, she tapped on one of the windows and waited, holding her breath. Tapping again, a fraction louder, she stepped back, ready to run if someone rushed out to angrily warn her off. Not a sound.

As well as the cottage, there were several outhouses, one of which could be a garage although it looked as though no one had used it for months, if not years. The shed next to it could have used for farming equipment. If the place had once been a farm. A smallholding perhaps, with chickens and goats and pick-your-own fruit and vegetables. The door to the shed was slightly ajar. Izzy touched it and the collection of old horseshoes and a pair of antlers, that someone had attached to it, rattled, making her jump back, scanning all around in case the owner had heard.

With a mixture of relief and disappointment, she turned and began making her way back to where she had left the car. It had been a chance in a million. Well, perhaps not quite such bad odds, but surely if Dawn had been there she would have come out, if only to ask about Cressy.

11

An evening with Harry and Janet was just what Izzy needed to take her mind off what had been going on. Kath had picked her up at seven thirty and during the drive, to what they both laughingly referred to as "Harry's country estate", the two of them had talked, mainly about the business and whether Harry was going to let them have a say in who he took on to help with the extra work.

Izzy had considered telling Kath about her trip to the country the previous day, but when she arrived at work Kath had insisted on discussing the possible reasons why Izzy had contracted a cold, even if it was only a mild one. Had she got a new boyfriend? No, of course not. Had she made it up with Josh? Definitely not.

All day, Kath had seemed on edge. But when questioned she had denied it. Now she had a new string of questions for Izzy.

'Have you been to see the baby again?'

'No.'

'Will you be going again, do you think?'

'I might. I like the family, especially Bev. We seem to be on the same wavelength.'

Kath gave a snort. 'Unlike us, you mean.'

'No of course I didn't mean that. What's the matter with you, Kath?'

'Nothing's the matter with *me*. If you want my honest opinion, Izzy, you're worried about your friend Dawn – I can understand that – and you're worried you haven't been in touch with the police. I can understand that too. And you're projecting all your worries onto me. You are worried, aren't you?'

'Not really,' Izzy lied, 'I gave myself a specific time in which to make a few inquiries and it's not up yet. After all, what's the rush? Cressy's in safe hands.'

'But is Dawn?'

'How do you mean?' But Izzy knew exactly what Kath meant. Someone who decided to leave their baby outside another person's house was, by definition, badly in need of help.

They were driving up a winding hill with trees that met overhead.

'If you're not sure what to do,' Kath said, 'think about what worked with Dawn before and I guess you could say the same method's likely to work again.'

'It's not like that, Kath. I don't know where she is. I don't even know for certain that Cressy is her baby.'

Kath puffed out her cheeks, slowly releasing the air. 'When Miles returned to his wife, Dawn must have been devastated. She begged him to come and see her – right – and wherever she was staying at the time she must have hoped she could persuade him to change his mind, especially now the baby had been born.'

'We don't know that's what happened.'

'But it sounds about right, wouldn't you say?'

'Yes, I suppose so.' Izzy had a sudden thought. What if Miles had known nothing about the baby, had not even known Dawn was pregnant? He already had a child, and he'd been through the tragedy of a baby that died soon after birth. If Dawn thought a baby would mean he ran a mile, she might have decided to get rid of it. Not kill it, even Dawn wasn't capable of something that terrible. But leaving it outside Izzy's house could have felt like the rational thing to do. Dawn had always been very persuasive, and her speciality was persuading herself she was in the right.

But Miles would have known she was pregnant.

'Listen, Kath, we have to make a go of this evening.'

'Yes, of course. What do you mean, make a go of it?'

'Oh, I don't know.' Izzy was not sure herself why she had made the remark. 'To tell you the truth I'm not sure why we've been invited. Anyway, Janet's a great cook and for once I'm starving.'

Janet welcomed them warmly. She was wearing jeans and a loose-fitting sweater that had seen better days, but there was nothing unusual about that. With a different hairstyle, she would have looked younger. On the other hand, why did women have to struggle to look younger than they actually were, dyeing their hair and taking steps to eliminate small wrinkles and lines? When Izzy grew old she was going to let nature take its course. That's what Dawn would do. Dawn had never worn make-up or changed the colour of her hair.

Since the children had grown up, the most important thing in Janet's life, after Harry of course, was her house and garden. During the winter months, she concentrated on the house, redecorating, putting up more shelves, renovating the kitchen. Harry often complained about the upheaval but in a good-natured kind of way, and Izzy suspected he was glad of his wife's practical skills. In the summer, she concentrated on her plants and now, even though it was the last day in October, the garden still looked good.

An outside lamp lit up the late-flowering cyclamen, surrounding a tree that had shed most of its leaves. Janet would have collected up the leaves for her compost heap. Next to the place where the compost was kept, a vine with crimson leaves wound its way up the wall. During the summer, Janet had shown Izzy and Kath round and, as far as she could remember, that was the last time they visited. Izzy thought the white flowers were a winter honeysuckle and made a mental note to tell Janet how beautiful they were. She liked Janet. When she'd started working for Harry, Janet had been very welcoming and friendly.

'Lovely to see you.' Janet showed them into the room that looked out on the lawn with its bird table and sundial. 'Harry's phoning someone but he'll join us in a minute. How are you both? Harry says he's taking on a new member of staff to ease the pressure a bit. High time, I'd have thought by the look of you two.'

She broke off, addressing her next words to Izzy. 'I'm so sorry about your alarming experience. How is the poor little thing, or don't they tell you once it's been whisked away into care?'

'She's fine,' Izzy said, 'I've seen her a couple of times and I'll be seeing her again tomorrow. She's in a very good foster home. Nice family with two teenage children, both being fostered long term.'

'Izzy's made a friend there,' Kath said. 'With the foster mother, I mean.'

Janet handed each of them a glass of red wine without asking if it was what they wanted. 'But what's going to happen to the baby? How long is it since it was found? Must be a couple of weeks. You'd think the birth mother would have been traced by now. I suppose she could turn out be psychiatric, not able to look after a young baby.'

'Yeah, but they'd give her some help,' Kath said, and Izzy thought about Bev's foster children, and their mentally ill birth mother, and the devoted way they were looking after Cressy.

Harry had entered the room. He was making an effort to appear cheerful, pleased to be entertaining them, but he had been in one of his moods all day and it was clear he was unable to shrug it off. Janet too seemed tense, ill at ease. Now that the conversation about the baby had come to an end, she was struggling to come up with a new topic, then Harry and Kath both spoke at once.

'Sorry.' Kath said.

'No, you carry on.' Harry poured himself a whisky. After a few drinks perhaps he would start to relax.

'I was only going to say how lovely the room looks.' Kath waved her had round. 'That's a new painting isn't it, Janet?'

Janet smiled. 'Yes it is. I remember how you liked the one in the dining room. This is by the same artist. He lives and exhibits in West Wales so it's quite a trek to see his work – but always worth the effort.'

The food was well up to Janet's usual standard. The starter was individual salads with a saffron dressing. Not too filling, Izzy thought. In spite of her comment that she was starving, most starters spoiled the main course.

Harry talked about the new car he was thinking of buying. 'Not that I'm one for flashy cars, but they impress the clients.'

'I'll bet,' Izzy laughed, 'what's wrong with the one you've got?'

Janet said nothing. Perhaps she thought the car an extravagance. When she began collecting up their plates, Izzy moved to help her but she waved her aside. 'Shan't be long. I'm bringing the next course in on the trolley, a chicken dish with thyme, garlic, and bay leaves.'

'Sounds amazing.' Kath beamed. 'Anything with chicken's great by me.'

The food was excellent – Janet must have been preparing it all day – and Izzy would have enjoyed it a lot if she hadn't felt so tense. Nothing to do with Dawn and the baby. It was the atmosphere in the room.

Normally, Janet had plenty to say, starting with what her two boys were doing, and leading on to her main hobby, apart from gardening: the amateur dramatic club she belonged to, and the play they were planning to put on.

'Delicious.' Harry wiped his mouth and placed his knife and fork together on his plate without making his usual clatter. 'What's next?'

Dessert was zabaglione with crushed amaretti biscuits. Izzy only knew because Janet announced it. The chicken dish had been a little too strongly flavoured for her taste but she loved desserts and this one was particularly mouth-watering.

'Well done, my darling.' Harry had relaxed a little, probably the result of the large meal. 'You're the best cook ever.'

'Yes, you are,' Kath chorused. 'I do my best but so many of my dishes go wrong.'

It was not particularly funny but everyone laughed. Then silence descended again.

They stayed on in the dining room for coffee, and the subject of the abandoned baby was raised again, this time by Harry, who wanted to know how the police were handling the case.

'They did the usual checks.' Izzy made an effort to sound less exasperated than she felt. 'I had a couple of visits from a police officer called Linda Fairbrother, but I got the impression they were only making sure no one accused them of not doing their job properly.'

It was just about the last impression Fairbrother had given her but Harry seemed to accept this. 'I admire you, Izzy. I'm not sure how I'd have reacted. I think I might have taken it personally.'

'How do you mean?' She knew exactly what he meant but was playing for time.

'Oh, forget it,' he yawned. 'The poor woman, whoever she is, had to leave it somewhere. Pure chance she chose your place.'

Kath started to cough. Like Wendy Bruton, it was something that happened when her nerves got the better of her. 'Hope I haven't caught your cold,' she told Izzy, 'I mean the one you thought you were developing.'

'I'll fetch some water.' Janet had jumped up and already reached the door. 'Don't try to talk, it always makes it worse. Shan't be half a tick.'

Kath soon controlled her coughing fit, but Janet's 'half a tick' turned into several minutes. Harry fidgeted impatiently, moving back his chair in preparation to rise then changing his mind.

'I'll go and help,' Izzy said, 'Janet mentioned she was going to make some more coffee.'

Out in the kitchen, Janet was leaning over the sink with her forehead resting on the taps. She seemed not to have heard anyone come into the room, but when Izzy spoke she gave no indication it had given her a fright. And made no attempt to invent an excuse.

'I'm sorry,' she said at last, 'what was it I came out for?'

'Are you feeling unwell? If you are, do say so, we can easily leave. There's nothing worse than having to pretend you feel fine when really –'

'I'm not ill.' Janet fetched a towel that was hanging over a radiator and dabbed at her eyes.

'Your winter honeysuckle is lovely.' Izzy was not sure she wanted to know what was wrong. It was probably some marital thing, the reason Harry had been in a mood. 'I used to think there was nothing to do in the garden in the winter months, but that's not right, is it?'

Janet sat down at the kitchen table. 'You know about it, you must do.'

'Sorry?'

'Don't pretend. Please don't pretend.' But when she looked at Izzy she must have realised she had no idea what she was talking about. 'Kath and Harry, it's been going on for weeks but I've kept quiet in the hope it would blow over.'

'Kath and Harry? Are you sure? What makes you think ...' But the first doubts had entered Izzy's head. Kath had been busier than usual, less inclined to want to go out for a drink. And quick to change the subject if Izzy said anything about Harry. Once they had gossiped about him behind his back in a good-natured kind of way. Recently any remarks Izzy had made, about the volume of work or Harry's bad-temper if a contract was creating problems, had been cut short. Not so much with a defence of Harry, just talk about graphic businesses in general and changing technology.

Janet was spooning coffee grounds into a jug. 'He's done it before,' she said flatly, 'I can't count the times.' But I'm afraid this may be more serious. Now Will's at college, Harry doesn't have to worry about the children. '

'How did you find out?' Izzy wanted the facts. Anger rose in her but she was ashamed to admit to herself that it was anger because Kath had kept something so important to herself, and allowed Izzy to tell her things in confidence which she now suspected she would have passed on to Harry. Or would she? Kath was no fool and clearly her main aim was to keep the affair a secret.

'A friend saw them together,' Janet explained resignedly, 'sitting in a pub holding hands. And in case you think there could have been a simple explanation, she saw them again, in the street, standing under a lamp post kissing like star-crossed lovers.'

The kettle boiled and Izzy started making the coffee. She found a tray on the side, and some cups, and a small white jug, and milk in the fridge.

'Thank you.' Janet took the tray from Izzy's hands and started moving towards the dining room.

'I'll talk to Kath,' Izzy promised, 'find out exactly what's been going on.'

'And then? If it's all out in the open, Harry may feel obliged to move out.'

'Better to know the truth.' Izzy wondered if some residual loyalty to Kath remained or she was on Janet's side. Not that taking sides was going to make any difference.

In the car going back, it was Kath who spoke first.

'You and Janet,' she said warily, 'you were out in the kitchen for ages.'

'Were we?' Izzy had no intention of making it easy for Kath.

'She knows.' Kath stared through the window at the darkness. 'She told you. God, what a fool I've been. All these weeks I've been busting to tell you but how could I? With the three of us working together, think how you'd have felt.'

'I guess I could have handled it,' Izzy said sarcastically, imitating Kath's American accent, 'but learning about it from Janet … What was I supposed to say?'

'We've always been so careful.'

'Not careful enough.' Izzy swerved to avoid a small mammal, a stoat or a weasel, that was making a dash from one side of the road to the other. 'You were seen in a pub and later standing in the street.'

'Where?'

'Pretty stupid, snogging in the street.'

'We want to live together. It's a question of waiting for the right time.'

Izzy gave a hollow laugh. 'It always is. What gets me, Kath, is the way you let me confide in you – about going up to Cheshire to see Dawn's mother, then visiting Miles' ex-wife – and all the time you were passing the information to Harry.'

'No that's not true, I swear it isn't. OK, so people sometimes indulge in pillow talk but I knew how important it was to you that no one found out. If what you were accusing me of was right, Harry would never have asked that question about the police being suspicious.'

Izzy shrugged. 'Once people start lying there's no end to the tricks they play. At least you could have told me before this evening.'

'How could I?' For the first time Kath sounded angry. 'You've always seen Harry as some kind of father figure, someone to go to if you needed advice.'

'No, I haven't.' But even as she spoke Izzy knew there was some truth in what Kath was saying. Harry was almost twenty years older than she was, safe, solidly reliable. How could she have been so naïve?

'People do have affairs.' Kath's voice was silly, like a spoilt child. 'You could never trust Josh, could you?'

'Thanks.'

'No, I wasn't being horrible. I was thinking of you.

You know I was. Only it did occur to me. No, that's crazy, how could it be?'

'Now what are you talking about?'

'The baby. Only Josh could have got some poor girl pregnant, then let her down, and she was getting her own back, leaving the baby with –'

'People don't give away their babies that easily.'

'No. No, of course not. Only if she was desperate enough and Josh had refused to accept it was his and she wasn't getting any maintenance for it.'

'By "it", you mean Cressy. I've already thought about this, Kath, confronted Josh with the possibility. I'd know if he was lying.'

But would she? Would she really? When they lived together she had told him about Dawn, let slip little incidents from their childhood. But not the game when they had to think of a name for their baby. Surely she hadn't told him that.

You're not listening, Miles. She came here, came to the cottage and had a good nose round. What did she want? I've made the situation perfectly clear. Fucking hell, Miles, do I have to do this totally on my own? Anyway, I've made a plan. No, don't look like that. A woman in the village stared at me. Listen, you cretin ... Oh, I'm sorry, my darling, take no notice. I'm just a grumpy old ... The plan – you want to know about the plan. Nothing you need to worry about. First I have to send this official-looking document to Izzy. What a laugh! These days you can fake just about anything. It's too easy, like taking candy from the proverbial baby. Miles is a funny name. Miles and miles and miles. Dawn is supposed to make you think of the rising sun. The dawn of a new age. Do you suppose my mother was making some kind of a joke? I am sorry, Miles, I really am. I know how much you worried. But it's all right now, isn't it, everything's going to be blissful. You and me, Miles, what a combination!

12

'Alan's taken Nigel and Pippa to a firework display,' Bev said, 'it doesn't start till it's dark but they're eating out – to turn it into a proper treat.'

'Did you want to go with them?' Izzy wondered if she should offer to look after Cressy for a few hours – or would that be against the rules? What rules? Surely foster parents were allowed to use babysitters.

'Not my kind of thing.' Bev tucked the baby into her buggy and began negotiating the space between the kitchen table and the back door. 'Besides it does them good to spend time on their own with Alan. Hang, I'd better bring a bag with a nappy. Just in case.'

They were going to take Cressy for a walk. The weather had turned colder but she was dressed in a fleecy suit that would keep out the wind. Her little face peeped out from her warm nest. Izzy tickled her tummy and she smiled.

'She smiled, Bev.'

'I know. Isn't she sweet?'

'So she must be about six weeks. Isn't that the age they smile?'

'Varies a bit, but yes. When you found her two weeks ago you thought she was three or four, didn't you? I think you were right.'

'When do they start on solids?'

'Oh, not yet. Depends. Around four months. The health visitors are always changing their minds. She's a contented little one so I doubt she'll need to start any earlier. Why do people make such a fuss about food? No, I wasn't thinking of babies. All those television programmes and once a mouthful's been chewed a few times does it make any difference what it looked like on the plate? People seem to talk about food far more than they used to. What is it, do you suppose, a substitute for sex?'

Izzy laughed. Presumably Bev was thinking how glad she was there was no evening meal to prepare for the others. Izzy was hungry, could have done with a sandwich, but the moment had past and Bev was locking the back door on the shopping that had been scattered over the kitchen.

Since the pavement was narrow, it was impossible to walk alongside each other until they reached the road that ran up to the park. Bev slowed down to let Izzy catch up with her.

'Lucky to live here, aren't we,' she said, 'even though our house is not exactly in the same bracket as these.' She nodded towards a large Victorian semi. 'You prefer the city, do you?'

'Not really. When I moved into my house I didn't know the area all that well. I suppose it was a way of trying to put down roots.'

'And did it work?' An old woman with a walking aid was approaching them. Bev seemed to know her, but as it turned out it was only someone she saw most days when she was taking Cressy for a walk.

'I lived with my boyfriend up to a few weeks ago,' Izzy said.

'Oh, I see.' Izzy could tell Bev was hoping to hear more.

'It wasn't working out. I told him to go but I'm not sure he's accepted I meant it.'

'All that to deal with, then Cressy left on your doorstep. No wonder you look a bit peaky.'

'Looking "peaky" means I looked bloody awful.'

'Rubbish, it gives you a kind of romantic aura.' Bev smiled to herself. 'Oh, take no notice of me. The reason I babble on, I don't get a chance for much adult conversation. With another woman I mean. Not the same with men, is it?'

'But you must have female friends.'

'A few but all the talk's of schools and moody teenagers.'

They had reached the park, with its wrought iron gates, and beyond them two rows of trees and a large expanse of grass. For the first time, Izzy wondered how far they were from the sea. She knew the way to Bev's house but had no mental map of the town in her head. Presumably if the seafront was reasonably close by, that would have been Bev's walk of choice. But perhaps not. Looking at the sea was a treat for people who lived inland, but not for those who lived in a holiday resort.

Bev sat down on a wooden seat and put the brake on the buggy. 'If they never find the mother, it'll be years before anyone's allowed to adopt. Unless the poor woman turns out to be dead.'

'Yes, I suppose that's right.' As in Kath's case, abandoned babies lost out all round. First their natural mother gave up on them, then they were denied a permanent long-term replacement in case she turned up out of the blue and demanded her child back. 'How far away is the sea?'

'Five minutes.' Bev pointed to a road. 'We could go back that way if you like, take a roundabout route. Come on. The weather's improved but not enough to sit down for long.'

If anything the wind had increased, but Izzy liked it by the sea when waves were whipped up and the boats bobbed up and down.

'We're spoiled,' Bev said, 'living at the seaside. When we first moved to Dawlish I thought we'd go to the beach every day, but you start to take it for granted and in summer it's too crowded, although Nigel and Pippa don't mind.'

'Where did you live before?'

'Exeter. Then Alan was transferred. In a way, I was sorry to move, but we're settled now. I've never asked you this before, but did the police think there was a particular reason Cressy was left outside your house?'

'Obviously it crossed their mind.' Izzy longed to tell Bev the truth. 'As I said before, my road's been pedestrianized so it was an ideal place to –'

'Yes, that makes sense.'

But Izzy knew she was as suspicious as DS Fairbrother. 'I did have a friend,' she began, 'but... I wish I could tell you more, Bev, but it's all guesswork.'

'You're saying you might know who the mother is? She could come back any day.'

'No. No, I doubt if she will.' Izzy knew what she was thinking. Without warning, the social worker could phone and say she was coming to collect Cressy. Nigel and Pippa had been prepared for this but the whole family was banking on being able to keep her, at least for a few months. Perhaps they hoped the mother had mental health problems, like Nigel and Pippa's birth mother, and Cressy would be placed in permanent foster care.

'It must be so hard for you,' Izzy said, 'not knowing what's going to happen.'

Bev gave her a look, as though to say, it would be easier if you told me everything you know. 'It's Nigel and Pippa I worry about.'

'Yes, but worse for you.'

'What makes you say that?'

Cressy had woken up and started to cry.

'She's not hungry.' Bev lifted her out of the buggy. 'Just wants to join in the conversation, don't you, Cressy? Would you like to hold her?'

'Yes please.' Izzy lifted the baby against her shoulder. 'Oh, you're right, she does feel heavier.'

'Than when you found her? They reckon she was probably an average weight when she was born, between seven and eight pounds.'

'How can they tell?'

'Well, I expect there's some guess work but full-term babies develop at more or less the same rate. By five or six weeks they can look at an object and follow it if it moves.'

'That's what she's doing now when you hold up her toy.'

'Pippa gave her that. Bought it with her pocket money. Do you suppose the poor soul gave birth to her all on her own? At least she was well cared for. And she's a little fighter. That's what they call them but I reckon all babies are programmed to fight to survive.'

'So she wasn't premature?'

'Full-term they think, the people at the clinic. She always has a proper check-up, just in case. They know what happened so they have a special interest. Everyone loves her.'

'I'm not surprised.' Cressy was snuffling against Izzy's ear and it brought back a sharp memory of that night when she had refused the bottle because the milk was cold, and Izzy had heated water in a pan and ...

Bev had gone silent. 'You'd like to adopt her,' Izzy said, 'I don't blame you. I wouldn't mind having her myself.'

'Really?' Bev's head spun round.

'No, I'm not serious, it wouldn't be right. What I'd like would be if she could stay with you and Alan.'

'Thanks.' Bev sounded close to tears. 'I can dream. Who knows, we might get home and find the social worker on the doorstep, come to tell us her mother's been found, alive and well.'

'Even if she had, surely she wouldn't get Cressy back unless she could prove she could give her a good home.'

Keenly aware of Bev's distress, she felt terrible that she had failed to air her suspicions, if not to the police, at least to Bev and Alan. But how could she? Inevitably, telling them would mean talking to the police. November the first. She would give herself another week then it would be impossible to keep it to herself.

Back home, Blanche had gone missing. Once it was dark she was usually curled up in one of her favourite places, but Izzy had searched the house and there was no sign of her. For an hour she waited, getting up now and again to look through the window or check the yard, opening the front door and calling Blanche's name. Cats often stayed out. It had happened once before when she was only five months old. Josh had panicked, gone tearing all over the place, only to return to the house at the same moment Blanche squeezed through the cat flap at the back.

By nine o'clock, Izzy was unable to stay in the house. One more check, to make sure Blanche had not slipped in unnoticed, and she set off down the road. No point asking passers-by if they had seen a cat, even though Blanche had a distinctive white coat. Best to check round the back where there was a patch of rough grass.

Half an hour later, she had walked up and down, peering under bushes and staring up into the branches of trees, without seeing any sign of a cat. Her biggest dread was that she would find her in the gutter, having been hit by a car. She turned corners, holding her breath until she had checked. At the bottom of hill, something was lying in the middle of the road, and she felt her heart begin to thump, but it turned out to be a supermarket bag, full of rotten fruit.

A familiar figure was coming towards her, familiar although it took her a couple of seconds to take in who it was.

'Izzy?'

'What are you doing here?' It was Stuart Robbins.

'I might well ask you the same.'

'I'm looking for my cat. She's gone missing.'

'Can I help?'

'Thanks, but I'm going home now. She may have turned up of her own accord. I need to check.'

He walked alongside her, crossing the road when she did and pausing at the top of her street so that she guessed he had known all along where she lived. Had he been coming to see her? If he had, why not say so, but if she had to describe him she would say he was a private kind of man who liked to keep his thoughts to himself.

'You look cold,' she said, 'would you like some coffee?'

'Coffee?'

'Up to you.' Izzy had her hand on the door, waiting impatiently. There was no need for him to sound so surprised, making her feel as if a simple offer of a cup of coffee was tantamount to asking him to stay the night.

'Thanks.' He followed her into the house. 'What kind of a cat is it?'

'She's white. I chose a white cat because I thought it would stand a better chance crossing the road.' Her voice was shaky with emotion. She hoped he hadn't noticed, but he had.

'I'm sure she'll turn up. Why not pour yourself a drink? When I was a kid, I used to get myself into a terrible state if a pet went missing or looked like it was on its last legs. On my ninth birthday, my rabbit died. I found it stretched out in its hutch and when I told Dawn she burst into floods of tears and insisted on making a wooden cross to stick over the place where my mother had buried it.'

He noticed Izzy's face and put his hand up to his forehead. 'I'm sorry, how stupid can you be. Stories like that are just about the last thing you want to hear.'

'No, no it's all right. Wasn't Dawn a bit young at the time?'

'Four or five, but people often imagined she was a good deal older. She was so solemn, like she had the whole weight of the world on her shoulders.'

'Yes, I know what you mean.'

He took the two glasses she was holding and filled them from the half-empty bottle of red wine. 'No news then? I thought you might have heard from Rosalie.'

'No, nothing.' Had he heard something and come looking for her to check out if she knew more than she was letting on?

The house felt cold, as though the central heating had broken down, but when she touched a radiator it nearly burned her hand. If only Blanche would come back. If only Dawn would contact her, explain why she had abandoned her baby, and say where she and Miles were living. But that would mean Bev had to give up Cressy. She had only looked after her for a couple of weeks but people were supposed to bond with a baby in minutes. No, that was their own baby. With someone else's it had to be different. However appealing the child was, a part of you had to hold back. Bev had fostered other babies, but in those instances she had known more or less for how long a period because the mother had been ill or homeless.

Stuart had moved across to the window and was looking out. 'Do you like living on your own?' He had his back turned but when she remained silent he turned to face her. 'Nice to have someone to come home to, but it's not that simple is it?'

'No.'

'Harry said ...' he began. 'I'll go when I've finished this and on my way I'll have another look round for your cat. What's her name?'

'Blanche.'

'How much has Harry told you about me?'

'Nothing. Just that you have an interest in old buildings. And the birds. Look, if you know anything about Dawn ... I know she's my friend but just now that's irrelevant, all that matters –'

'I don't,' he said firmly. 'If I did, I'd have told you. Are the police looking for her?'

'She's not a missing person, not in their terms. If she wants to steer clear of her family and friends that's up to her.'

'How's the baby?'

'Doing well. Actually I saw her this afternoon.'

'Really?'

The surprise in his voice annoyed her. Surely, if he had been the one to find Cressy he would have wanted to make sure she was all right. But perhaps a man would feel different. Perhaps Cressy had awakened something in her, a wish to have her own child. With Josh? Imagine what a disaster that would have been.

After Stuart left, she went out again, walking fast towards the city centre, but taking a route Stuart was unlikely to know, through the maze of pedestrianized streets. She had given up calling Blanche's name. Cats weren't like dogs. They responded to the sound of a tin being opened but only rarely to their names. She was wondering what Stuart had been going to say when he started talking about Dawn and, as she walked, one morbid thought followed another. The cat she had found dead at the bottom of their garden. Stuart's rabbit. On both occasions, Dawn had wanted a proper funeral with prayers and hymns and bunches of flowers.

She loved rituals, which partially explained why she had joined the cult in Scotland, although Izzy had always imagined the kind of community where people felt free to express their feelings. Dawn had never said much, either about why she had joined or why she had left, but a few months after her 'escape' the leader had fled to South Africa amid allegations of financial irregularities.

Izzy was walking fast, trying to keep warm, but it wasn't just that. Someone was following her. For some time, she had sensed it, now she was sure. Who was it and what did they want? Surely not Stuart. Supposing it was Dawn, angry because Cressy was in foster care? But Dawn was unlikely to have followed her surreptitiously. Dawn confronted people, forced them to do what she wanted.

Thinking she heard footsteps, she spun round but there was no one. Then, a few moments later, she spun round again and was certain she spotted a shadowy figure disappear into a doorway. Should she go and check? It could be someone who wanted to steal her phone. She wanted to run but that would only draw attention to her and let her assailant know she was afraid. What assailant? She was becoming paranoid, and if she was she had brought it on herself.

She dreaded returning home, and finding Blanche was still missing, but she could hardly keep touring the city all night. Turning left, then left again she started back to the house and it was then that the obvious explanation for Blanche's disappearance came to her. Why on earth had she failed to think of it before? It was something he had threatened to do but she had never believed he meant it. Josh loved Blanche, thought of her as *his* cat. He was the one who had taken her.

13

Blanche was still missing. It wasn't Josh. Josh would not be that cruel. He would have come round, carrying the cat, talking in a baby voice. *Me and Blanche want to come home to little Izzy, don't we, pussy cat?*

Monday, and her work at the office was piling up. Harry had been patient. Now that she knew about him and Kath he needed to be. But he was aware her mind was not on her work and his patience would end if she made a serious mistake. They were designing a holiday brochure for someone who had built ten wooden chalets on a piece of land near Dawlish Warren. Izzy had seen the chalets and they looked a lot better in the advertising material than they did in reality. Never mind, it wasn't her job to criticise the owner or the photographer who had taken the pictures. Her job was to make sure the brochure lured holidaymakers from the Midlands. People who had checked out the website and clicked "Please send me a full colour brochure".

Dawlish Warren had two halves, the crowded part with food outlets and shops that sold buckets and spades – and the bird-watching area. She thought about Stuart Robbins and his work with birds. She should have asked him to tell her more about it. They had discussed Cressy, and Dawn – she had taken care not to connect the two – and Blanche, but she had taken little interest in his work. He probably thought her self-obsessed and had only helped her search for her cat because it would have been callous not to. Either that, or he had sensed she was keeping something from him and was determined to discover what it was.

She had returned from work convinced Blanche would have come home, but the cat food was untouched. An hour spent searching all the places she had been to before had been a waste of time. She had known it would be but done it just the same, like a ritual to appease the gods. Please let Blanche come back and I'll never ... Never what? She was too depressed to care and it was not until after seven that she bothered to collect her mail from the mat and was surprised to discover it wasn't all junk. A handwritten letter had a Cheshire postmark and even though she had not seen it for more than ten years, Izzy recognised Rosalie's spidery scrawl.

The letter was a long one. Izzy skimmed it to try to discover if it contained anything important then decided she had better read it carefully from the beginning.

Dear Isabel, she read, *it was kind of you to come and see us and I know you must be as worried about Dawn as Francis and I are. You were such a good friend to her in Chester and again when you joined her in London. If she hadn't met Miles I feel sure she would have settled in Exeter, at least until she had completed her Ph.D. I blame myself that she ran away to Portugal. I think Miles must have given her the security she lacked as a child. At least that's what I told myself at the time. But something I didn't tell you when you came to see me – shortly after their return to this country she wrote asking me to lend her some money. She gave no reason so I assumed Miles was having difficulty finding a job although surely he could have signed on unemployed. Anyway, to cut a long story short, I sent her five hundred pounds – it was all I could manage – but since then I've heard nothing, although the cheque was cashed. If you write or get in touch in any other way please don't mention this to Francis. He's not a mean person but he thinks children should stand on their own two feet – I haven't told him much about the past – unless it's a matter of life and death. If you hear anything – anything at all ... I'm not on the phone – you know how I've always hated them – but get in touch. You know you could have stayed with me and Francis but I think I can understand why you preferred to get a good night's sleep before you faced us. How you must miss your dear father. Oh, just one thing. Dawn once accused me of lying to her about her father. Why would I want to do that, but she got into her head he was some kind of romantic hero – I suppose children often do that – when in fact he was a perfectly ordinary businessman. Your parents were so good to us but it's hard to accept charity however well meant. Next time you're in touch with Sylvia, do give her my best. Dawn was so fond of her and I sometimes think other people's parents are easier to get on with than your own. It must have been strange for you, seeing me and Francis. together. Derby and Joan – isn't that what they say? You know the expression "the love of my life"? I think it's right, you get one chance and if you fail you have to live with the consequences for ever. All the best, Rosalie.*

P.S. You remember when Dawn was thirteen she had to take time off from school with a virus? Did she ever tell you what really happened? I was so ashamed.

Izzy read the letter twice, then a third time, when she

underlined the slightly ambiguous parts. The remark about how hard it was to accept charity – *however well meant*. And the part about it being easier to get on with someone else's parents. But the most alarming bit was the postscript. Dawn had missed nearly a month of school with a virus. What *had* really happened, and why had Rosalie been so ashamed?

She had added a PS, saying Francis had just come home with one of those awful mobile things. She included the number and said if Izzy called, Francis would answer as she, Rosalie, would have no idea which button to press.

Why did she behave as though she lived in another age? But she had always been set in her ways, something Dawn had often complained about. *Your mother's more broad-minded, Izzy. I think mine would like me to take holy orders.* Not true, as it turned out. Rosalie had been dismayed when Dawn joined the community in Scotland.

Did she expect an answer to her letter? Izzy decided to wait a week or two in the hope that she would have something to tell her.

What would she do if she found Dawn? How could she decide when she had no idea what was going on in her life? Did she want to find her? Cressy was in a home where she was loved and wanted and Izzy dreaded the thought of her being returned to the person who had abandoned her.

Someone was standing outside the window, looking up. Izzy peered through the crack in the curtains and recognised DS Linda Fairbrother's bulky shape.

Opening the front door before Fairbrother had time to ring the bell felt like a way of getting the upper hand. 'Come in.'

'Thank you. I called earlier but there was no reply.'

'I was looking for my cat,' Izzy told her. 'Incidentally,

what would happen if someone took her to the police station?'

'We check if it has a chip then pass the animal on to the shelter. Have you tried them?'

'No cat answering her description.'

'I'm sorry.' Fairbrother sounded as if she meant it. 'Wish I could help. I'll ask around but you know what cats are like. Probably wandered off too far and can't find its way home.'

'That's not what cats are like,' Izzy said irritably.

'No? I've never had one myself. Too much of a responsibility when I'm out so much.'

Izzy sat down. 'Is there any news of the baby's mother?'

'The mother?' Fairbrother's tone of voice implied Izzy had asked a rather surprising question.

'That's what you've been working on, isn't it?'

'Cressy,' Fairbrother said, 'Cressida, shortened to Cressy. When you found the slip of paper in her carry cot, didn't it strike you as an unusual name?'

'Fairly.'

'You know other Cressidas?'

'No.'

Fairbrother took a notebook from her pocket and flicked through the pages. 'You've lived here for three years, is that right?'

'You asked me that before.'

'And up to a few weeks ago, you shared the house with Josh Lester.' She looked up and noticed Izzy's exasperated expression. 'Just checking to make sure I haven't slipped up on anything.'

Izzy sighed. 'How does who I used to live with have any bearing on the case? Oh, you think Josh was so pissed off I'd asked him to move out, he decided to find a stray baby and leave it on my doorstep.'

'You're feeling depressed.' She made it sound like a statement rather than a question. 'About Mr Lester? I know what a trauma it can be, ending a relationship. What happened? He found someone else?'

'No.'

'Yes, you're right, nothing to do with us, no bearing on the case at all. As I said before, we have to check every possibility, can't take anything at face value. My only aim is to reunite the baby with her birth mother, or if that's not possible, social services can fix her up with a more permanent home.'

'She's fine where she is.'

'You've seen her again? When was that? Goes a bit beyond the call of duty, doesn't it, driving all the way to Dawlish.'

'If you ask me the best thing that could happen to her would be if she stayed with Bev and Alan.'

Fairbrother drew her teeth over her upper lip. 'If only life were that simple. Anyway, I doubt you'll be hearing from me again so I'll love you and leave you.' She stood up then paused, looking up at the ceiling. 'If I hear of a cat … White one, you say?'

'She's called Blanche.'

Fairbrother nodded. 'Cressida. Pretty name. You know, withholding information from the police is a serious matter. Any information, I mean, however unimportant it might appear. Over two weeks since you found her on your doorstep. Normally, we'd have heard something by now. The mother would have turned up or someone would have come forward with information.'

'So what will you do now?' Izzy could feel her heart thudding. Was it so loud, Fairbrother could hear it?

'Of course, it's always possible someone's shielding

the mother, someone who in their misguided way thinks she's doing the right thing.'

Izzy was too tired to think. Her head felt muzzy and all her limbs ached. Switching on the living-flame fire, she crouched close up to it then froze when she heard noises coming from next door. Someone coughed and she thought she could hear footsteps on bare boards.

In a matter of seconds, she was out in the yard, looking up at the house. A light was flickering, either a torch or a candle. Had the electricity been cut off or was there someone inside who had no business to be there? The person who had been following her when she searched for Blanche?

Her first instinct was to ignore what she had seen. There couldn't be much for a burglar to take, although she had heard of people who stripped houses of all their fittings – Victorian fireplaces, ceiling mouldings, even stair rails. Access to the house was impossible from the back. Quite apart from that, knocking on the front door would be safer and give her a better chance of escaping, should whoever was inside turn nasty. Not that someone up to no good was likely to respond to the knocking. Perhaps she should call the police, but it would only add to Fairbrother's suspicion. *Is there something you're not telling me, Izzy? Withholding information from the police is a serious offence.*

Outside in the street, no lights were visible in the house. She bent down, pushing her fingers in the letter flap, listening. Had she imagined it or could she hear whispering?

'Is anyone there?' Her voice echoed in the empty hallway, which must be the mirror image of her own. 'I live next door. I was just wondering if everything was all right.' She sounded ridiculous. Whoever was inside would have his hand over his mouth, trying not to laugh. Or planning an escape over the wall at the back. Then she heard footsteps coming closer.

When the door opened, Izzy was standing a few paces back from it, but the light from the street lamp illuminated the girl's face.

'Jade?'

'What are you going to do?' The girl's face was flushed. 'We're not doing any harm. I promise. There's nowhere else to go. I thought it would be all right. Are you going to tell my mum and dad? They're –'

'Hang on, Jade, I just wondered who was walking about.'

'Yes, I know. I'm sorry, I should have –'

'Where are your mum and dad?'

A fair-haired boy, dressed in a white T-shirt and torn jeans, had joined them. He opened his mouth to speak but Jade gave him a shove and told him to shut up.

'They've moved to London,' she said.

'Yes, I know. The house is up for sale. I heard noises and thought someone had broken in. But you're still living here?'

'No. Yes. I'm finishing my A-levels. Mum arranged for me to stay with a friend of hers in Heavitree.'

'And you kept the key to the house. '

Jade pointed to the 'For Sale' notice. 'Nobody's bought it – not yet.'

'Must be freezing,' Izzy said, 'or have you fixed up some kind of heating?'

'Sleeping bag,' the boy explained.

'I see.' Izzy smiled. Their faces were so deadly serious. 'Well, as long as you're both all right. By the way, you haven't seen my cat, have you?'

'Blanche?' At the change of subject, Jade relaxed

154

visibly. 'Has she gone missing? We could help you look for her. This is Kieran. You wouldn't mind searching, would you?'

'Sure.' He was a good-looking boy, a little older than Jade perhaps, but he seemed pleasant enough. His clothes could have done with a wash but his hair had been cut in the latest style so presumably the scruffy clothes were part of his image.

'I thought maybe Blanche had slipped in when you opened the front door' Izzy said, 'but you'd have seen her, wouldn't you, and she'd have asked for food.'

'Poor Blanche.' Jade looked almost as worried about her as she had about Izzy discovering their love nest. 'She could be in someone's garage or garden shed but if she'd got shut up somewhere she'd have made a noise, wouldn't she, unless she'd been injured. Oh, I do hope she's all right.'

'Anyway, I'll leave you to it.' Izzy said. 'I only checked because I thought it might be burglars.'

'It's our last evening,' Jade said sadly, 'Kieran's going to France to stay with his father. It's all right, the day after tomorrow I'm going back to where I was staying before.'

'Good.' Izzy turned away then changed her mind. 'Actually, can I come in for a minute, Jade? No, nothing to do with the two of you camping here.'

'Yes, of course, but there aren't any chairs.'

'You probably haven't heard about it but someone left a baby outside my house.'

'A baby?' Jade's hand shot up to her face. 'When? I didn't know. Oh God, how awful. What did you do? Was it –'

'She was fine, in good health. You didn't read about it in the local paper, or I suppose it could have been on TV.'

'No, nothing.' Jade turned to Kieran. 'You didn't see

anything, did you?'

He shook his head. 'Who could have done something like that?'

Jade clutched at his arm. 'The mother must have been desperate. I'd love to have a baby, wouldn't you? They're so sweet.'

Kieran was frowning. 'I did see this old man outside your house. I don't suppose he had anything to –'

'When? What was he doing?'

He shrugged. 'That's just the thing. He was stroking a cat, a white one, then he gave it some kind of treat from his pocket. At least, I thought it must be a treat. Do they have cat treats? I suppose they must do. The stuff you can buy for pets – it's crazy.'

'Can you remember any more, Kieran? Did he pick Blanche up?'

He shook his head. 'Old man with an old pram. Looked like a tramp.'

'Had you seen him before?'

He shook his head again. 'Actually I'm not even sure the cat was white. It was dark, difficult to see properly so it could have been one those tortoiseshell ones. Anyway, Jade and I'll have a good look round later on.' He jerked his head in the direction of the kitchen. 'We bought some takeaway and –'

'And now it's going cold.'

Jade was twisting a lock of hair round her finger. 'And you won't tell my mum and dad.'

'I don't know their address or phone number, Jade, but I'm trusting you to return to your friend's house tomorrow. Just one last thing, Kieran. The old man with a pram. Did you see his face?'

Kieran thought about it for a moment. 'No. Actually, I sort of half saw it. It was strange. I'm not quite sure why but it made me think it could be a woman.'

Later, Izzy checked online for any cottages to let near The Railway Inn. She should have thought of it before but it had only occurred to her while she was talking to Jade and Kieran. When she discovered the cottage, where she hoped Dawn might be living, there had been no 'To Let' sign, not that there would have been much point, since it was so far off the beaten track, and in any case, the place looked in no fit state to let.

14

Izzy was trying to remember Dawn's address before she left for Portugal. She had never visited her there – Dawn had never invited her – but she had an idea it was in Heavitree. Jade telling her she had been living in Heavitree had reminded her, and she cursed herself for not thinking of it before. Not that it was likely to be much help.

After a long search, that reminded her how much her place could do with a good clean, she found an old diary and was fairly sure the address scribbled in the back was the right one. It was worth a try. On the few occasions they had seen each other, Dawn had insisted on coming round to Izzy's house or that the two of them meet up in a pub. In fact, she had been so unwilling for Izzy to visit where she lived that Izzy had thought there must be something or someone she didn't want her to see.

Had Miles lived there with her? Dawn had told her so many lies and half-truths it was impossible to remember when and where she had met him. The affair could have been on and off, while he plucked up the courage to tell Wendy he was moving out.

Dawn had said he was living in a bedsit, but no location had been mentioned and it could be that he had lived in Exmouth until they left for Portugal. He would have missed Dominic and Dawn would have been less than sympathetic. Did she have some hold over him, or had things between him and Wendy been so tense he had fallen into the arms of the first woman who showed an interest in him? That made Dawn sound unattractive, which was certainly not true, but any man who became close to her would soon have discovered just how determined she could be. Determined to get her own way.

Parking near the hospital, Izzy checked her street map and began walking back to the cul-de-sac off Heavitree Road. It was highly unlikely Dawn was living there, and also unlikely anyone living there now would know where she was. When they met up in Exeter it had nearly always been in a café in the shopping centre. Once, Izzy had looked up Dawn at the university and they had eaten lunch together in the canteen, but Dawn had made it clear it was not something she wanted to repeat. At the time, Izzy had expected to be introduced to other students, but as far as she could tell Dawn had made no friends. Was it always the same if you were doing a higher degree? Did you carry out most of the work on your own? She had asked Dawn about her thesis and Dawn had muttered something about 'comparative religions and personality.'

'Do you mean people with particular personalities are more likely to be attracted to particular religions?'

Dawn had shrugged, not wanting to talk about her thesis so presumably, at the time, she had been more interested in her affair with Miles and had only turned up at the university when she had to see her supervisor. The way things were going, it seemed unlikely she would ever complete her degree. But how unimportant all that was now. With a sinking feeling, Izzy realised she was beginning to think she might never see Dawn again. If the parcels and messages stopped arriving would that mean she was dead? No, if that happened they would find her body. Unless she had done something, or gone somewhere, in order to make sure no one ever did.

Checking the number on the slip of paper in her pocket, she banged on the door – there was no bell – of number nineteen. After more knocking, and a wait that felt like a couple of minutes but was probably less, she was about to give up when the door opened a crack and a cross-looking young man stood there, dressed in pyjama bottoms and a university sweatshirt.

'Yes?' It was just after midday – Izzy's lunch hour – but she guessed she had dragged him out of bed.

'I'm sorry to bother you but I'm looking for a friend of mine. Dawn Dear.'

A strange look passed over his face. 'She doesn't live here.' The door started to close but she put her foot in it.

'I know, but she used to. Look, I wouldn't have come if it wasn't important. Only I think she may be ill. Or even in danger,' she added, determined not to leave without finding out as much information as she could.

The student rubbed his eyes and gave a heavy sigh. 'I suppose you'd better come in.'

'Thanks.' She followed him down a dark passage, stepping over a pile of junk mail and a sports bag, and negotiating the narrow space between a bicycle and the wall. 'I'm really sorry to get you out of bed but it's the only address I've got for her. She went abroad –'

'To Spain.' He rubbed his unshaven chin. 'No, Portugal. But I guess she came back.'

'What makes you say that?' They were standing in a surprisingly clean and tidy kitchen, a large room with a table and four chairs as well as the usual sink, cooker, and fridge. 'She's been in touch with someone who lives here?'

He shook his head. 'Been round. I'm the only one left who knew her. I say knew her but she never had much to say for herself. I doubt we exchanged more than a dozen sentences. When she left, she must have had a spare key cut.'

'To this house.'

'You said she might be in danger, or was that just a way of persuading me to let you in. By the way, I'm Rhys.'

'Izzy. It's a long story but –'

He shook hands. 'It's OK, no need to tell me all the details. A letter came for her. I didn't know what to do with it. She'd left no forwarding address so I thought maybe I should open it, return it to the sender. Is that what you're supposed to do, or is it against the law, interfering with somebody's mail?'

'I don't know. I expect so. What did you do?'

He poured himself a glass of water. 'That's the thing. I left it on that shelf by the front door while I thought about it. It was handwritten, not junk mail, looked personal. Only, a couple of days later, it disappeared and Joe – he's on the top floor – said he'd been looking out of his window when this girl with long hair – fair hair – came up to the house. He thought she must be delivering flyers or something, then he heard her put a key in the door, but when he came down to check she'd gone.'

'Lots of girls have long fair hair.'

'You don't think it was Dawn? It was addressed to her so –'

'Thanks, you've been really helpful.'

'What makes you think she's ill? Or in danger. What

kind of danger?'

Izzy hesitated. 'When I said ill, what I meant –'

'I get it.' He stood up and switched on the electric kettle. 'Some kind of mental breakdown. It wouldn't surprise me. She's kind of odd, isn't she? If I'm honest, I tended to give her a wide berth, keep out of her way. Or did you mean she's in trouble with the cops?'

'She's a friend of mine, used to be. No, it's all right, I know what you mean. Actually I'm here on behalf of her mother. She's worried about her, hasn't heard from her for months. If she comes back –'

'I shouldn't think that's very likely.' He covered the remains of a dish of lasagne with a plate. 'But if she does I'll say you called round. Izzy. Does she know –'

'Yes, but I'll write it down just in case.'

'What shall I say you wanted?'

'Just tell her I need to talk to her. I'm sorry, for all you know ... I'm not the police and I'm not from social security or the tax office.'

He laughed. 'I believe you. Cup of tea?'

'No, thanks. Yes, all right, if you're having some. Thanks.'

'Sleepless night?'

'Do I look that rough? It's not because of Dawn. I've lost my cat. I've been searching for ages. Yes, I know, only a cat but –'

'You love him. Or is it a her?'

'Blanche, she's called Blanche.' And to her horror, she started to cry.

History never repeats itself. Not exactly. Izzy was watching a programme about whales, without taking anything in, when she heard sounds coming from next door, then wails and someone banging on her door. Racing to the front door, she wrenched it open and found Jade. She was holding Blanche who was so dirty she was barely recognizable, and there was an open wound on the back of her neck.

'Oh, Izzy, look at her. Poor thing, she could hardly walk.'

Gently carrying her into the house, Izzy laid her down on one end of the sofa and began stroking her head. Normally Blanche would have purred, but she was too exhausted, or too badly injured.

'I heard mewing,' Jade said. 'I thought it was a baby. Is she all right?'

'I don't know.' Supposing she had come home to die? Just made it before she gave up and stopped struggling? Her coat was matted and one of her paws was curled up as though it caused her pain to straighten it.

'She's glad to be back,' Jade said, and Izzy managed a weak smile.

'Yes, she is.'

'Perhaps she's hungry. She looks quite thin.'

Izzy fetched a pot of Marmite – Blanche hated milk but was addicted to Marmite sandwiches – spread a little on her finger and held it to the cat's mouth. Blanche took a cautious lick, tried to stand up on the sofa, and wobbled over again.

'It's all right, Blanche.' She was afraid to pick her up again in case it hurt her. Would there be a vet on call through the night? If there was it would be expensive – even daytime consultations cost the earth – but what did that matter? But when she inspected the wound, she could see it wasn't a deep one, and apart from her injured paw, Blanche was not in as bad a shape as she'd feared.

Ten minutes later Blanche was sitting on the floor, washing, and had even managed a few husky purrs. Where had she been? Had someone taken her, or had she been hit by a car, crawled away to safety and stayed there until she felt stronger?

But a much more alarming possibility had occurred to her. If Josh had taken her he would never have let her get in such a state. Unless she had run away from where he was living. No, whatever Josh's failings, he wouldn't have stolen Blanche.

The phone started ringing and she left Blanche with Jade. Tender loving care was what the cat needed just now and Jade seemed to be an expert at that. In the morning Izzy would take her to the vet for a proper check.

'Yes?' As soon as she answered the call, she had heard a strange sound, half a wail, half a laugh. 'Who is that?'

No answer.

'Dawn?' Izzy glanced at Jade, but she was fully occupied inspecting Blanche's paws. 'Is that you, Dawn? Please speak. If you're in trouble, I'll help. Please, Dawn.'

Could she hear breathing, or was it Blanche's purrs?

'Dawn? Are you still there? If you tell me where you are I'll come and see you. It'll be all right, we can ...'

But like the last time, the line had gone dead.

Jade was watching her now, pleading with her eyes. 'Kieran's gone.'

'I'm sorry, you must miss him, but you'll see him again, won't you?'

'I kept a key to the house. Just in case. You won't tell my mum –'

'I told you I wouldn't.'

'You might have Mum's mobile number.'

'You won't let me down, Jade. Promise?'

Jade gave Izzy a hug. 'I absolutely, definitely promise. Thank you so much. And I'm so glad Blanche is all right. Izzy?'

'Now what?'

'That phone call – was it one of those people who want to sell you double glazing or something?'

'Nobody spoke.'

'But sometimes they put lots of calls through and only speak to the one who answers first.'

'It's a possibility.'

'But you think it's something to do with the baby.'

'I don't know, Jade.'

'Is there anything I can do to help?' Jade looked so worried; Izzy couldn't help grinning.

'It's kind of you to offer but the police are trying to trace the birth mother and the baby's doing well. She's in a foster home in Dawlish.'

'Oh.' Jade rubbed her eyes. 'Only Kieran thought the old man with the pram might have something to do with it.'

'Really? I don't know how he worked that one out. Look, I'd tell you everything I know, but I don't want you caught up in –'

'So there is something? I knew there was. I think it was someone who knows you'd look after the baby. I mean, if it was a stranger she'd have left it in a public place, a health centre or a bus station. 'Cos she left it during the night, didn't she, and no one would have seen her. Only it's cold in the night so I'd have thought she'd have chosen somewhere indoors.'

'All these questions have gone through my mind too, Jade. Best to leave it to the police.'

'Yes,' she said doubtfully. 'I wish you'd tell me what you think but I know you're not going to.'

After Jade left, Izzy phoned Stuart. There were questions she needed to ask – about Dawn, and about Rosalie – and this time she was going to refuse to take no for an answer. If Dawn was as violent as Stuart had hinted, she could she have injured Blanche deliberately and made sure Izzy saw what she had done. *If you don't get Cressy back ...*

Stuart's phone rang at least ten times. *Come on, come on.* Then, just as Izzy thought it was going to click into answerphone, the ringing stopped and an out of breath woman said, 'Hello?'

'Oh.' Izzy had planned what she was going to say. Now she had to make up some excuse. 'I ... The thing is I belong to a bird-watching society and we wondered ... It's all right, I'll call back another time.'

'Shall I give Stuart a message? If you tell me your number ...'

'No, it's all right. There's no need.' She was talking too fast, giving herself away. 'It's not urgent. Sorry to bother you.'

My birthday, Miles. My twenty-ninth. Rather a romantic idea, never reaching thirty. Would Izzy see it that way, do you suppose? You know, Miles, you haven't been very reasonable. After all, I could have harmed Dominic. No, of course I wouldn't – I love children – except they do say some rather stupid things. My mother once said I was like an adult once I'd reached the age of eight or nine. Does that make sense? There was a boy who owned a rabbit and my mother thought it might have germs, make me ill. I don't think pets are a good idea, do you? I mean, Cressy might be allergic to the fur, and they're not very hygienic, always licking their genitals. Are you listening, Miles? I'm only spraying this air freshener because the place smells of damp. When I said I was going to tell Wendy about Cressy, you threatened all kinds of silly things. If you want my opinion, that was a little over the top. After all, you knew I didn't mean it, you knew it was only because I love you. The trouble is, you could have meant it. While I was asleep you could have crept downstairs ... Then what? Knives are messy. Blood means clothes have to be disposed of, even carpets. My love is like a red, red rose. Love you, Miles, love you, love you, love you, yes I do.

P.S. You were right about Izzy. I mean, I was right. Was it my idea or yours? Never mind, it's all for the best. That boyfriend of hers is a total idiot. He'll fit in with whatever she wants.

15

Kath had come round but it wasn't clear why. Just a social call? It didn't feel like it.

'So Blanche is OK. That's brilliant. I wonder where she'd been. Must've got lost but they say cats always find their way home.'

'Not if someone drops them off in another part of the city.' Izzy regretted her remark as soon as she had made it since it was bound to lead to more questions.

'Who would do that? Oh you mean kids – for a joke. Some kind of joke! Listen, the reason I dropped by, I know you've been worrying about the baby and what's happened to her mother but I was thinking, she could have moved on, be miles away.'

'It's possible.' Izzy was exhausted, wanted to go to bed, but it was only ten thirty and Kath would think she was ill. 'Look, it was nice of you come and make sure Blanche was all right, Kath but –'

'That's not why I'm here.' Kath sat down with a heavy sigh. 'I know how you feel about me and …'

'You and Harry.' So this was the real reason for her visit. 'I don't feel anything, Kath, it's your life, up to you.'

'He'll never leave Janet. How could he? Men his age hardly ever leave their wives. Do you think he will?'

'I've no idea. Probably not.'

'Why d'you say that?'

'They've been married for God knows how many years – and there's the house. Harry loves that house.'

'More than he loves me,' Kath said sadly, 'no, it's all right, that's what I think too.'

'I'm sorry, Kath.' Izzy was so tired her eyes felt blurry. 'Listen, I promise not to criticize but in exchange I need your advice and it means trusting you not to pass on –'

'Scout's honour.'

'It's important, Kath.'

'I know. I can tell. Fire away. Anything that takes my mind off my own problems.'

Half an hour later, Izzy had given her an account of her friendship with Dawn over the years and Kath had listened carefully, commenting occasionally that she sounded a pretty crazy kind of character.

When she told her about the name Cressy she let out a small gasp. 'You think ...'

'The thing is, Kath, I gave myself a week to try and find out more and it's up. It was up several days ago.'

'So you're going to tell the cops.'

'Yes. I don't know.' Kath was wearing too much perfume. For Harry's benefit. 'What do you think?'

'I guess you'll have to. If you don't you could land yourself in serious trouble.'

'She threatened to kill herself if I did,' Izzy said, and Kath pulled a face as if to say, oh, that one.

'You don't think she means it?' It was a question Kath couldn't possibly answer. How could Izzy expect her to, and how could she be so feeble, hoping for reassurance when she was the only person who could decide what to do?

'Blackmail,' Kath said. 'Still, I don't know this Dawn. If she's unstable ...'

'She's cunning but that's not the same thing.'

'No, it's not.' The description of Dawn had certainly taken Kath's mind off Harry. She looked much more like her old self, quite cheerful, quite animated.

'She also implied I would be in danger myself.'

'Not if she'd killed herself. Sorry, I guess it's no laughing matter. Listen.'

'What?' She hoped Kath had some sensible advice for her, half hoped she would insist on accompanying her to the police station.

'When you split up with Josh ... How did you do it? It's so difficult. I – you're stronger than me and once you've made up your mind you stick to things, carry them through.'

'If you knew how hard it's been. How hard it is. No, I don't want him back but having him around, I was used it. We all miss familiar things and –'

'So how did you do it?'

'I'd put it off, and put it off, but finally ... He was ruining my health.'

'Body or mind? Both I guess. Yes, I know what you mean. My stomach's terrible, I've completely lost my appetite, and I feel so guilty. So many conflicting feelings and –'

'When it gets bad enough you'll do something about it.' Izzy wished she could sound more sympathetic. 'What has Harry said? Have you asked him?'

'No. I don't know. Don't want to know. Don't tell the police, not yet. Imagine how awful it would be if Dawn killed herself. You'd never get over the guilt.'

So the part about Izzy being in danger had gone over

Kath's head. No Josh. No Kath. She had never felt so alone. Bev Jordan would have been a comfort but how could she tell her about Dawn then insist she keep quiet?

And if I was Bev, she thought, in the circumstances, would I keep quiet? Probably not. Cressy was her concern. Not Dawn. Bev dreaded Cressy being returned to her birth mother but she would do anything to protect her.

Izzy was watching a programme about two boys who had been taken abroad by their Turkish father, and their mother had spent more than three years getting them back. So much of it was a re-enactment, it was confusing when actual photographs of the parents and children were shown, and she remembered how people phone crime programmes, claiming to have seen a suspect, when all they've spotted is the actor who played him.

When the doorbell rang, she had a nasty feeling it might be DS Fairbrother, so it was a relief to find an elderly man standing there.

'Oh.' He looked her up and down as though she had no right to be living there. 'I'm looking for an Isabel Lomas?'

She should have said 'who is it who wants her'? Instead, she asked if he was a colleague of Fairbrother's. His mystified expression persuaded her he was not a policeman. Besides, they retired in their fifties, didn't they – with a substantial pension – and this man looked more like he was in his late sixties, or even seventies. 'Yes, I'm Isabel Lomas.'

'Good to meet you.' He held out a large, slightly moist hand. 'We've never met but you'll recognise the name. I'm Graham Dear.'

'Graham Dear,' she repeated stupidly.

'Dawn's father.'

'But I thought –'

'I was dead. I know. That's what Rosalie wanted everyone to believe. Much easier that way. Wipe me out of her life entirely. Never to darken her door. I assume you know Rosalie.'

'You'd better come in.' He could have been anyone, but he knew Dawn's name and it appeared he was telling the truth. Or was it a trap? 'How did you know where I lived?'

'Dawn told me.'

'Dawn did? When? You know where she is.'

'Some time ago. In a letter. She said it was in case anything happened to her. Why would she have said that, do you imagine? The more I think about it the more worried I become.'

As well as knowing Dawn's name – and Rosalie's – there was the shape of his face. And his eyes. Family likeness is such a strange thing. Sometimes, someone's walk is identical to the way one of their parents' walks. Or a hand gesture, a smile. But in Graham's case it was the eyes, which were slightly watery but unmistakably the same very bright blue that in Dawn's case gave her such a striking appearance.

He sat down without being invited to and she offered the usual drinks that were waved aside. 'I'm returning to Liverpool tomorrow, but I decided to stop off in Exeter in the hope I might find you at home. I called round once before but you were out.'

'I can't understand why Dawn gave you my address? All along, she's known you were alive and ... You've seen her quite recently?'

He shook his head. 'At one time she was hoping to stay with you for a while. Am I right?'

'She never said.'

'No? You were close friends when you both lived in

173

Chester. And there was the money, although in the end she wanted me to send it to her old digs in Heavitree. Rather risky I thought but she insisted.'

'Did she tell you why she needed it?' Izzy was still taking in the fact that he was alive. Was he really Dawn's father? Were his bright blue eyes sufficient to convince her? He knew about Chester too but that would not have been too difficult to discover.

'Oh yes, no subterfuge there. She was expecting a baby. No remorse. No regrets, although she refused to divulge the name of the father so I assumed he must have done a bunk. Of course the whole thing could have been a lie. The pregnancy, I mean. Just something to tug at the heartstrings.'

'How long is it since you saw her?'

He thought about this. 'Four years, could be five. Her mother never knew we'd kept in touch. It was Dawn's idea and when she contacted me – she must have been fourteen at the time – I jumped at the chance. She didn't tell you?'

'Not a word.' At the time, Izzy had thought Dawn told her everything. That's what close friends are supposed to do. It wasn't true. 'Where did you meet?'

'You're checking up on me. I can't say I blame you. That café near the river. What was it called? Not Ye Olde Tea Rooms. Something like that. Aunt Carrie's tea room? No, not Carrie. What was it?'

'I don't know. It doesn't matter.'

'And in case you still don't believe me, Dawn was fond of your parents, particularly your doctor father, and you have two brothers, and you attended art school. You see, we used to have quite a chat. At one time, Dawn intended to study medicine. I encouraged her, even offered financial help, but all to no avail. The religious fever took over. A great shame, I always thought.'

So he knew about her own family too. Izzy was a little unnerved by that, but of course Dawn would have told him whatever suited her. 'Our little secret – that was how she liked to see it when we met.' He fingered his wiry moustache. 'Always a one for secrecy, but I don't imagine I need to tell you that. She'd let her mother think she was going to the library or some such story and we'd have a cup of tea and a fry-up. Rosalie disapproved of fried food.'

'Yes, I remember,' Izzy laughed, 'I hate to think what she'd have done if she'd found out.'

'You've been good to her. To Dawn, I mean. That's why I was hoping you'd know where she is now. And whether there actually is a baby.'

What should she tell him? Not very much. Certainly not about Cressy. 'I've been looking for her myself,' she said, 'I know she came back from Portugal with Miles, but she hasn't been in touch. I checked with the university, but they knew nothing. Hoped I'd be able to give *them* an address. I expect she owes them money.'

'I'm sure she does. Oh, she came back all right, that's when I got the letter asking for a substantial amount of cash. Did she tell you she was having a baby?'

'No. We're not that close now. No arguments or anything but she'd changed – the community in Scotland I expect – and we had less in common than we used to.' Blanche had woken up and stretched. Now she was approaching Graham.

'Ah, a cat. I like cats.'

'She was in an accident. No, it's all right, she's almost recovered.'

He thought about this, putting out a hand to gently stroke Blanche's head. At least, Izzy assumed that was what he was thinking about but in fact it was Dawn.

175

'She's never been easy.' He spoke with a mixture of regret but perhaps a little pride. 'Such a clever child. Don't know where she got it from, although Rosalie's more sharp-witted than she appears. You knew her and her mother well. Her best friend, I believe. In which case you'll remember she had a short temper. And a cruel streak. The bruises on her mother's face.'

'You mean ...'

'If you do happen to bump into her please ask her to get in touch with me. Would you do that?'

'Yes, of course.'

He took a small notebook from his coat pocket, tore out a page, and scribbled an address and phone number. 'Will you tell Rosalie I've been in touch?'

'No.'

'Best not.' When he closed his eyes and threw back his head, she guessed he was trying to work out whether or not he believed her. 'No doubt I was cast as the wicked father, the deserting husband,' he said. 'It wasn't quite like that. If you know Rosalie ... But there's no point in going into all that now. The past is the past. How is Rosalie these days?'

Izzy was silent. She had no wish to lie to him. On the other hand, the less she said the better.

'There are things I could tell you ...' He broke off, rubbing his hands together. 'Not now. As I said –'

'If I see Dawn I'll ask her to contact you.'

'Yes, please do.' He stared at her and she knew he felt she was holding something back. Should she tell him about Cressy? Explain that she had no proof but ... Then she would have to mention the parcel and notes. He would leap on the information as proof that she really had been expecting a baby. He seemed as concerned about Dawn's well-being as she was, but any information she gave him

176

would mean he contacted the nearest police station straight away.

'Thank you for agreeing to listen to me.' He stood up and shook hands. 'I'm sorry I've involved you, particularly the part about the pregnancy, but I couldn't think where else to go.'

She glanced at the slip of paper he had given her. 'You still live in Liverpool then?'

'I do. How does Rosalie explain my death?'

'Some people seem to think you were killed in an accident.'

He looked at her expectantly, wondering perhaps if, since she clearly accepted he was who he said he was, she might be prepared to tell him more. 'As I said, I'm returning home tomorrow. Stayed the night in a bed and breakfast place near the station. Don't worry, you won't see me again. But don't lose my address and phone number, will you?'

When Kath banged on her front door, Izzy had been fast asleep. Now she was wide awake.

'How did you find out?' she asked, but Kath shrugged the question aside.

'Never mind about all that now.' Kath was concentrating on driving the short distance to the hospital even though there was virtually no traffic about. 'A friend of a friend. Someone who thought it would be better if I broke the news to you.'

'You were at home at the time?'

'Yes. No. I'd been home earlier then I decided to go to that club down by the river.'

'With Harry?' So *that* explained the outfit she was wearing.

'No, of course not. It felt better than spending every evening mooning around feeling sorry for myself. Don't worry, I haven't been drinking. One glass of wine, and someone knocked my arm and most of that ended up on my top.' She pointed to the stain. 'I had no idea Josh was going to be in the same place.'

'So you weren't with him?' Kath had often remarked on how good-looking he was.

'With Josh? No, of course not.'

'I thought the two of you might have decided to drown your sorrows together. You say he fell in the river. So presumably he'd been drinking heavily.' Izzy felt slightly hysterical, wanting to laugh because the accident sounded so typical, but afraid his injuries might be more serious than Kath realised.

As they turned into the hospital car park, Izzy told Kath she could drop her off and she would walk home.

'As if I would.' Kath stifled a yawn. 'I'll wait in reception and drive you back.'

'I might have to stay quite a long time.'

'I doubt it. I don't imagine his injuries are that bad. If you decide to stay, you can ask someone to give me a message. Don't worry, I'll be fine. Give Josh my best wishes.'

16

He was in a ward on the first floor. Izzy was relieved but also a little irritated that, according to the nurse there was nothing to be alarmed about. So her visit could easily have waited until the morning. Had Kath overreacted or was it Josh's idea that she rush to his bedside?

'You're his partner?' the nurse inquired.

'No. Yes. I was.'

'He was lucky there was someone on the spot who knew some first aid.'

'But he'll be all right?'

The nurse gave her a reassuring smile. She looked very young but already she was in charge of a ward of patients all through the night. 'The river's none too clean, and he had a high level of alcohol in his blood. He was complaining of dizziness and nausea so we kept him in, but yes, he'll be fine.'

Josh was lying on his side but when she came close to the bed, he opened one eye and rolled onto his back. 'I was afraid you wouldn't come.'

'How are you?' The lights had been dimmed and the patient in the next bed, an elderly man with a white beard, was snoring lightly.

'Did Kath tell you I was pushed?' Josh spoke too loudly, then glanced at the elderly man and lowered his voice a little. 'I keep explaining someone was trying to kill me but nobody takes any notice. Who could have done it? You don't know anything –'

'You were drunk, Josh. And it's not the first time it's happened. Some idiot's always falling into the water.'

'Part of the reason I wanted to see you, Izzy ... I knew I'd be able to make you understand what happened. God knows, I can tell the difference between standing too close and losing my balance, and feeling a hard shove in my back.'

'What were you doing on the quayside?' She sat on the edge of the bed then changed her mind and found a chair. 'It gets crowded down there. I expect someone lost their balance and bumped into you.'

'No, no,' he protested, 'it wasn't that crowded. We'd gone to the club, been there three or four hours, then someone, I think it was Simon, said he needed some fresh air.'

'How many of you?'

'Five or six, I forget, but there were other people by the river too.' He closed his eyes. 'A bloke exercising a dog. Some crazy guy, pushing an empty pram. Listen, they're not going to keep me here long but I'll have to take some time off work. Only the thing is, Dave's flat's so bloody uncomfortable I wondered ... You heard what the nurse said. They wouldn't have kept me in unless it was serious.'

'No.'

He sighed. 'God, you're hard.'

'It wouldn't work, Josh, you know it wouldn't.' Was it possible he had engineered the 'accident' as a means of worming his way back into her life? Surely he wouldn't go that far. 'You must have other friends who'd give you a bed for a week or so. What about that person you work with? What was his name? Mark? Martin?'

He was pretending to be asleep. Izzy reached out a hand to smooth his hair then thought better of it. He smelled of disinfectant or perhaps it was floor of the ward. 'You could have drowned,' she said.

'I know. You'd have liked that, wouldn't you?'

'How's your head?' She had expected to find him swathed in bandages but all she could see was a small pad, held on by three strips of sticking plaster.

As she stood up, his eyes jerked open. 'Izzy?'

'I'll phone the hospital tomorrow – to find out how you are.'

'You're not coming at visiting time?'

'I expect they'll have sent you home by then. You don't seem too bad and there's always a shortage of beds.'

'Home,' he said bitterly, 'don't make up your mind without sleeping on it. Promise?'

'Sleeping? I'm not going to get much sleep now, am I? I'll think about it.'

'Thanks.' He blew her a kiss and from his expression she knew he had taken her words to mean she was going to give in. 'My head's throbbing like hell. Do you think it'll leave a scar? Some women like scars, find them rather romantic. I read about it in a magazine.'

'Bye, Josh.'

'Thank you for coming.' He stretched out an arm. But by then she was well out of reach.

'He's convinced he was pushed,' Izzy told Kath. 'At least that's what he tried to persuade me.'

'Someone did it for a laugh? How stupid can you get?'

'Did you see what happened?'

'Me? I was still inside the club. This guy came running in, said there'd been an accident, someone had been pulled from the river and his name was Josh.'

'How did he know his name was Josh?'

'Search me.' Kath accelerated as the lights changed to green. 'I suppose he could still talk. He can swim, can't he? Must have been bobbing about in the water.'

Izzy tried to picture the scene. Josh and his friends, standing on the quay side, laughing, jostling one another, chatting but with nobody listening, all pissed out their heads. 'Who was with Josh? I need to know, Kath. He's asking to stay at the house until he's well enough to go back to work but if I let him past the door –'

'The usual crowd. No one in particular.'

She was lying. Izzy could tell. 'He'd been chatting up some girl? There was an argument? The girl's boyfriend thought he'd teach him a lesson?'

'How would I know?' Kath protested. 'If I did I'd tell you. What do you plan to do?'

Izzy ignored the question. 'A bloke exercising a dog,' she said, 'and an old man pushing an empty pram. Did you see an old man?'

'Sorry, you've lost me.'

'Josh said those where the only people down by the river, apart from his friends.'

'An old *man* with a pram? Are you sure he didn't mean Queenie? You know Queenie, she goes through the shopping centre like a bat out of hell. Old pram full of heaven knows what. Not stray cats, nothing like that, I reckon the pram's like a security blanket, something to hang onto.'

'So what was she doing down by the river at two in the morning?'

'Maybe she's nocturnal, sleeps in the afternoon and early evening.'

'Who carried out the first aid?'

'Someone from the club. I expect Josh exaggerated. I doubt if he was in that bad a state.' Kath pulled up next to the kerb and waited for Izzy to climb out of the passenger seat. 'Sure you're OK? If you're still feeling shocked I could come in, stay a bit.'

'I'm fine. Sorry you had to leave the club early.'

'Oh that.' Kath sounded thoroughly depressed. 'Stupid idea in the first place. What did I think was going to happen? I'd meet this fantastic guy who'd sweep me off my feet and hey presto, Harry would be ancient history?'

'Have you talked to him?'

'What about? Oh, you mean living together. Didn't need to. You were right as usual, he'd never leave Janet.' She sighed. 'You like Janet, don't you?'

'Yes, why wouldn't I?'

'The way she dresses, it's not surprising Harry –'

'Oh, for God's sake, Kath, why can't she dress how she likes. I suppose it was you that persuaded Harry to have his hair cut.'

Kath sniffed loudly but Izzy was past caring if she had upset her. She still hadn't forgiven her for carrying on a secret affair in the office beneath her nose.

'That time I thought you and Harry were whispering about me ... I realise now –'

'You haven't contacted the police?' Kath blew her nose loudly.

'You know I haven't.'

'Well you ought to. No, sorry. Oh, I don't know what you should do. Only I was thinking ... No, it's a stupid idea.'

'Go on.'

'It just occurred to me … If Josh's right and he really *was* pushed into the river it could be an ex-girlfriend.'

'You mean someone he was seeing when he was living with me. You're not still thinking the baby's Josh's?' But no idea could be dismissed out of hand. 'You mean the mother dumped it outside my house because she thought Josh was still with me and wanted him to take some responsibility?'

'No, I guess that doesn't make too much sense. I mean, Josh would have admitted it. Surely he would.'

But would he? He wanted to get back with her so he was hardly likely to admit he had made another woman pregnant. If only she could trust him – to tell the truth. But he never had, preferring to tell her what he thought she wanted to hear. But his own child. Would he turn his back on his own child? From everything she knew about Josh that was the last thing he'd do. Let the mother do most of the childcare, fail to keep up with his financial contributions. But his own son, or daughter. He would show it off like his finest achievement.

'What's on your mind?' Kath asked.

'Nothing.'

'Liar.'

'See that shop over there? They sell sushi. I like sushi, don't you?'

'Shut up, Izzy, that wasn't what you were thinking about.'

Kath's suggestion that Josh was the father of the baby was absurd. How could she even consider it when there was no doubt in her mind that Cressy was Dawn's. And the old man, or was it a woman, with a pram. What was that all about? Jade's Kieran had mentioned the same thing. The person who she thought was following her, that time she was searching for Blanche?

Josh's behaviour, trying to persuade her to look after him as a way of returning to her house, was outrageous, but also typical. What was not plausible was Josh's girlfriend leaving her baby outside Izzy's house.

'Oh, by the way,' she said, 'Dawn's father turned up.'

'What?' Kath let out a shriek. 'I thought he was dead.'

'So did I.'

'What did he say? What did he want? Tell all.'

Izzy hesitated. 'Oh, just to ask if I knew where Dawn was living. He's as much in the dark as I am.'

'But if Dawn thinks he's dead ...'

'She doesn't. They used to meet up – in secret – when she was a child, in Chester. Her mother never knew about it. Or if she did she decided to keep quiet. Dawn asked him for money and he sent a cheque to her old digs in Heavitree.'

'When?'

'I'm not sure. Not long ago.'

'I don't like it, Izzy, I don't like any of this. You could be in danger.'

'Me?'

'Yes, you.'

When she tried to open the front door it stuck on something the other side. A large brown envelope had been pushed through, the kind that has a cardboard backing to protect the contents from getting bent, although in this case whoever delivered it had decided to get it through the letter box come what may.

Izzy carried it upstairs and dropped it on the bed. She was bursting for a pee and her head ached. In less than five hours' time she would have to be up and about again. Would she drop off or would she lie awake with Josh's words go round and round in her head? *Don't make up your mind without sleeping on it.*

Back in her bedroom, Blanche was curled up in a ball. Hearing sounds, she stretched out and began licking her bad paw. It had almost got better and it was best to let cats lick as their wounds. Something to do with their saliva having healing powers.

Izzy stroked her head then sat down next to her and struggled with the sticky tape on the envelope. Since all it contained was a single sheet of headed paper, why bother with all the sticky tape and the cardboard backing?

The letter heading had the name of a firm of London-based solicitors: Rimmer, Seavings and Bourne. They appeared to have an office in a part of London Izzy knew reasonably well, but the address meant nothing to her. She had never heard of Glossop Street.

"Dear Ms Lomas," she read, *"this is to confirm that you have agreed that in the event of Ms Dawn Dear's death you are prepared to become guardian to her daughter, Cressida."*

There were several more lines of legal jargon, and a space at the bottom for her signature, together with the date. No space for a witness to her signature. No stamped, addressed envelope so the 'document' could be returned. And surely, if you signed something you kept a copy. But the whole thing was so amateurish it was not worth splitting hairs.

Izzy held it up to the light. The paper was thick, the kind lawyers use, but it bore no relation to a legal document. In the morning she would go to the library and check if Rimmer, Seavings and Bourne existed. Not that it would mean much even if they did. Anyone could pick a firm at random.

Dawn had typed it and delivered it by hand, but she

couldn't possibly expect Izzy to accept it was a genuine document. All the same, the contents of Dawn's mind was starting to make sense. For reasons Izzy could only guess at, she had wanted her to have Cressy. To keep her, not to hand her over to social services. Convinced that Izzy would want to bring her up, the only explanation for what Izzy had done was because she believed she had no legal right to her. Now Dawn had provided her with the proof she needed.

Did Dawn think Josh was still living in the house? In Dawn's mind, had another reason for Cressy being given to foster parents been because Josh had turned nasty, dug in his heels, and forced Izzy to choose between him and the baby?

Picking up the envelope the so-called legal document had come in, she studied the label on the front, handwritten, not typed. It smelled odd – literally. What was the smell? Something musty but it wasn't just that. With a pencil, and so close to the edge of the envelope it could have been rubbed away in the post, someone had drawn a picture of a stag's antlers.

What was it Dominic had said? Something about a deer? But Izzy had thought it referred to Dawn's name. At least Dawn was alive. Or was she? If the letter was not from her, who else could have sent it. Dawn's father, Graham? Rosalie?

17

'So what happened, Josh? You chatted up someone's girlfriend and they clobbered you?'

'Do you mind?'

'All right, you slept with someone's wife.'

His hand moved up to his injured head. 'If there'd been anything like that I'd have told you.'

'Like hell you would. Anyway it makes no difference.'

He lifted his legs off the floor and stretched out on the sofa with his head propped up on two cushions. 'Have you thought it over?'

'Oh, I did that all right. You could at least have phoned me at the office, not just hung about till you knew I'd be back and arranged for the taxi driver to drop you off at the end of the road.'

'I thought they'd keep me another day,' he said, 'and I couldn't go back to Dave's.'

'Why not?'

He sighed, pulling the sides of his denim jacket across his chest and chattering his teeth although the room was pleasantly warm. 'I told you, because it's so hellishly uncomfortable. Hey, I've just thought, have you found someone else? Is that what this is about? You were always a fast worker but –'

'There's no one else.'

He smiled to himself. 'All right, I know when I'm beaten. It was nice of you to come to the hospital. I suppose it made me think you might still care.'

'Stop it, Josh.' What really got to her was the way – once he had decided he was wasting his time – he would leave, virtually unscathed, and throw himself on the mercy of some other female, or return to Dave. She, on the other hand, would be left feeling heartless, confused, regretful, angry, and upset. 'The baby,' she said.

'Sorry? Oh, you're not still worrying about it. Nothing to do with you. Could have been left anywhere.'

She stared at him, a cold, hard stare that made him flinch.

'What? You don't honestly think –'

'Whoever pushed you in the river could have been bearing a grudge. Or her husband could.'

'Do you mind?' He had his outraged expression. 'I never mess about with married women. You actually thought the baby could be mine? What's happened to you, Izzy, you're not thinking straight. No, I'm sorry, you've been through a tough time. We both have. If the baby was anything to do with me I'd have told you. You know I would.'

He was right. He would. How much easier it would have been if she could tell the police it was her ex-boyfriend's baby. But it wasn't. Cressy belonged to Dawn.

Someone was hammering on the door. Izzy ran to open it, and found Jade, in tears.

'Come in. No, it's all right, Josh was leaving anyway.'

'Was I?'

Even the sight of a distraught Jade was not enough for

him. 'Go, Josh!'

'But you've still got some of my stuff.'

'All right, go upstairs and put it in these.' She handed him two polythene bags, the kind she never normally used but last time she went shopping she had forgotten to take her cloth one. 'And the minute I've finished talking to Jade you're leaving.'

'I'm so sorry.' Jade found a tissue and held it to her nose and eyes. 'I didn't realise Josh would be –'

'Sit down. When I said he was leaving, I meant it. We split up weeks ago but he won't take no for an answer. What is it, what's happened? Is it something to do with Kieran?'

Jade shook her head.

'Your parents?'

She shook her head again and fresh tears rolled down her cheeks.

'Come on, whatever it is, it can't be that bad. Is it something to do with the house?'

Jade took a second tissue from the pocket of her jeans 'You know I said I loved babies –'

'Oh, Jade. Oh, I'm sorry, but you mustn't panic. There's things you can do. Have you talked to Kieran? Oh, no, he's not here. When you get in touch with him –'

'No, no, you don't understand.'

'What then? You're not pregnant?'

'I thought I was, I was so worried, but it was a false alarm. I've been so stupid, Izzy, we both have, only it wasn't Kieran's fault because I told him I was on the pill.'

'And you weren't.'

'No, but I am now, only what's the point 'cos I'll never see him again.'

'Why? Of course you will.' Izzy gave her a hug. 'Sit down and I'll make us both a hot drink.'

'When he left –'

'You told him you thought ... But you can text him, phone him. Tell him the good news.'

'If it is good.'

'Yes, of course it is. You're only ... How old are you? Seventeen – it's far too young. Listen, when I've made the drinks I'm going to let you in on a secret but only if you promise not to tell anyone.'

'I absolutely promise.'

'And I'm not even sure if what I think has happened is true.'

'Please tell me.' Jade accompanied her to the kitchen. 'Is it about the baby outside your house? If you know who it belongs to you, we have to help her. The police would take the baby away and say she was unfit. I've read about it. They take the baby away and the mother never gets it back. Think what it must be –'

'I'm not sure it's quite like that.' Izzy had no intention of telling her the whole story, just the bare bones, the suspicion that she might know who Cressy's mother was.

'I'd never abandon my baby, would you? The mother must be mad. No, I don't mean that. What I mean, she must have been so desperate she wasn't thinking straight. Only crazy people always want to be found out. That's why they leave clues. Did Cressy's mother leave any clues?'

With a thudding sensation in her stomach, Izzy remembered the scribbled drawing on the envelope from the fake solicitors. Stag's antlers. A deer. Dawn Dear. Or did it have something to do with the stag's antlers, attached to the door of the shed next to the cottage?

'Listen, Jade.' Izzy switched off the kettle. 'Can you come back later.' She lowered her voice to a whisper. 'After Josh's gone.'

192

'Yes, all right, you wouldn't mind?'

'To tell you the truth I need someone to talk to. But it'll be in complete confidence so –'

'Yes, of course. I absolutely swear.'

'See you later then. In about twenty minutes.'

As she let Jade out of the house, someone was coming down the road and as he drew closer he raised a hand in greeting. It was Stuart Robbins.

Josh was upstairs. She needed to get rid of him but there wasn't time. Better to put Stuart off, arrange to meet later if that was what he wanted. Why had he come? To explain about the phone call when his girlfriend had answered? There was no need. She had been grateful for his help, searching for Blanche, but any idea she might have had that the two of them ...

'Hi.' He had seen her and Jade standing outside the front door. 'You're busy.'

'No, no I'm not. This is Jade. She used to live next door.'

'But she's leaving,' Jade said. 'I'll see you later, Izzy. Let me know when you're free.'

'I was in the area,' Stuart explained. 'It was you that phoned, wasn't it? I expected you to call back but –'

'Don't worry, it wasn't important. In any case, how did you know it was me?'

'My sister-in-law answered. She was staying the night on her way back from Cornwall, where she'd been to see her father. You should have left a message. I'd have called you back.'

Izzy had been considering denying making the call but that would be silly. She had phoned, hoping she might be able to ask a few questions about Dawn's childhood and about Rosalie whose letter, as yet, remained unanswered. 'I just needed to talk to you about Dawn's father?'

Blanche had come to the door and Stuart was inspecting the wound on her neck. It would be several weeks before the fur grew back. 'Glad she turned up all right. Been in a fight, had she?'

'I've no idea. She could have been hit by a car. She's almost back to her old self.'

'Good. That's a relief. Are you going to let me in then? Any news of the baby's mother?'

'Nothing.' She stood aside, holding her breath, willing Josh to stay upstairs.

'As far as I can recall, Dawn's father was some kind of businessman, but that can cover so many activities.' He took off his coat and hung it on a hook. 'My father had an idea he might have killed himself. Some people see suicide as something shameful, reflecting badly on those around the victim who should have seen it coming.'

'Is that what Rosalie told your father?'

'Could have been. Why? It was a long time ago. I doubt if Dawn can remember him.'

'He turned up on Monday,' Izzy said.

Stuart looked surprised. 'Really? Here, at your house?'

'Obviously, I'd never met him before, although I'd seen a photo, but that was taken years ago. At first, I wasn't sure I believed him, but he knew so much about Dawn, and Rosalie, and my family. He told me he and Dawn used to meet in a café, in Chester, in secret. Rosalie never knew.'

'I wonder why she preferred to let everyone think he was dead.'

'A few months ago, I'm not certain exactly when, Dawn wrote, asking her father to lend her money.'

'That's what he told you?' Stuart's hand was enclosed by all four of Blanche's paws. He manoeuvred it free and stood up, crossing to the window at the front. 'So he knows where she is.'

'No. That's why he called round. She gave him an old address and went round there later to collect the cheque. She must have kept her key, or had a new one cut.'

'You're guessing all this?'

'No, I spoke to a student who's living there now. A woman with long fair hair was seen the same day the letter to Dawn disappeared from the shelf where it had been left. Also, I heard from Rosalie a week ago and Dawn asked her for money too, but that was when she was still in Portugal.'

She was searching in a drawer for Rosalie's letter. When she found it she gave it to Stuart, watching his face as he read. Could she trust him? For all she knew, he might be in touch with Rosalie and the two of them might be planning ... What was she thinking? For a split second, she wished she had handed the whole thing over to the police. Cressy was safe, but Dawn could be planning anything. The more she thought about it, the less she understood why the baby had been left outside her house. The fake letter from a firm of solicitors was mad. Dawn would know she would see through it immediately.

Supposing Miles had said he would stay with her, but not if she kept Cressy. No, that made no sense. He loved Dominic – that was one thing Wendy Bruton sounded totally sure about – and nothing she had heard about Miles led her to think he would have chosen Dawn over his own daughter. On the other hand, how could he tell Wendy he had a daughter when their own baby – a girl – had died soon after she was born?

If only she had taken more notice, the one time she met Miles. If she knew him better she might have some idea as to how he was likely to behave. Dawn could manipulate people. Was Miles a manipulator? She doubted it. On the other hand, Dawn could have pushed him too far. Then what would she do? What was the worst thing anyone could do to punish someone who refused to fit in with their plans? *Some people see suicide as something shameful, reflecting badly on those around the victim who should have seen it coming.*

Stuart folded Rosalie's letter and handed it back. He was wearing jeans and a thick grey sweater speckled with black, and he looked solid and reassuring. She was just about to offer him a drink when she heard a dragging noise upstairs. Josh searching for his possessions? Surely he would have the decency to keep quiet until after Stuart had left.

'The postscript,' Stuart said, 'did Dawn tell you why she was off school so long with a virus?'

'I think I assumed it was something like glandular fever.'

He continued to stand by the window. There was a full moon. Perhaps he was watching a flock of birds. Did they fly in flocks at night?

'What is your job exactly?' she asked. 'You carry out research, do you, how many birds of which species live by the estuary, what they eat, where they go in the winter?'

'You're interested in birds?'

'Yes. I don't know very much. I believe there are lapwings and avocets on the mud flats. Is that right?'

He gave her look that said 'you're not really interested, you just want to know if I can help you in your search for Dawn.' 'I've thought about it,' he said, 'tried to remember if anything was said, but nothing comes back. I lived nearby when Dawn was a young child, but you know her far better than I ever did.'

'If something unpleasant happened, my mother liked to protect us from it. If it didn't fit in with the nice, safe

196

world she had created.'

'You're saying you think Dawn did something bad? What kind of a thing?'

'I don't know.' Izzy thought she could hear a tap running. 'I don't think her father does either.'

'But her mother —'

'Rosalie would never tell me.'

He turned round, smiling. 'Are you going to tell me the truth about what's been going on the last two or three weeks.'

Josh was coming down the stairs, yawning. He had taken off his T-shirt and had a towel round his shoulders. 'Just washed my hair,' he explained. Then, pretending to be surprised. 'Oh, sorry, I didn't know Izzy had a visitor.'

'This is Stuart.' Izzy was shaking with anger. 'He knew Dawn before she and her mother moved to Chester.'

'The famous Dawn.' Josh sat down, still rubbing his wet hair.

'Josh had an accident,' Izzy said. 'He came round to tell me he'd recovered. He's leaving now.'

'Am I? No rush, is there? What's your line of country, Stuart? You live in Exeter, do you?'

Stuart was moving towards the door. Izzy opened her mouth to say again that Josh was just about to leave. It was a waste of time. How could Josh be so thoughtless? But it wasn't thoughtlessness: he had done it on purpose. A punishment because she had refused to let him back into her life. Why didn't she just tell Stuart the truth? But it was too late.

Just before he started down the road, Stuart glanced back at her and she knew, from the expression on his face, what he was thinking. *If you were living with someone, why on earth did you let me think you were on your own?*

Dearest Miles,

By now Izzy will have been in touch with the right people and arrangements will be under way, just as we intended. After all, one has the right to make whoever one pleases a guardian of one's child. I looked it up in the library. Very badly explained, by some cretin in the civil service I suppose, but they do at least spell out the letter of the law.

My mother once read a book – I think it was called The Bad Seed *– all about a girl who had inherited criminal genes, or perhaps I should call them psychopathic genes. Anyway, my mother must have been so afraid I'd inherited some from my father that she was determined to knock me into shape. And when I say "knock", I mean literally. God know, Miles, I've given Izzy enough help in my time. She always had an obstinate streak but I knew how to handle her, still do. I have ways and means, as they say! When she realises what's likely to happen, she'll get a grip of herself and do as she's told. If not – well, that doesn't bear thinking about does it, Miles.*

Love you always, Dawn.

P.S. There's a robin on the holly tree outside the window. Once I saw a dead one. A cat had got it. It could have killed a sparrow but it had chosen a robin. Some cats deserve what they get. And some people too.

18

'I'm worried about Dominic.'

'Has something happened?' Izzy was with Wendy Bruton, in a café near the river, quite close to where Josh had fallen in – or been pushed.

'He hates Miles,' Wendy said, 'told me he'd like to kill him. He's been having bad dreams, nightmares. Normally I would never let him sleep in my bed but –'

'He's upset, and not knowing where his father's gone must make it worse. Where is he now?'

'At a friend's house. A friend from school. He didn't want to go but I made him. You think I'm too hard on him, don't you?'

'Why do you say that?'

'It's the impression I get. You think I frightened Miles away.'

'No, of course I don't. It's never crossed my mind, and as for Dominic I'm sure it's best if his life carries on as normally as possible.

'He thinks Miles doesn't love him, but he does, I know he does. That day he went out and never came back … He must have gone to see Dawn. I'm certain he did.

Something to do with the phone call. She must have threatened him. Or persuaded him. Is she the type who –'

'Yes.'

'But he'd have been in touch with us – if not for my sake, for Dominic's, he adores him.'

'Where do *you* think he is?' She could hear church bells. It reminded her of the day she had visited Rosalie and Francis, not long ago but it felt like an age.

'I think he's returned to Portugal.' Wendy pushed aside her cup. 'She must have convinced him he ought to be with her, not us. Men are like that. If women put enough pressure on them they give in – for a quiet life. Miles hates arguments.'

Izzy sipped her tepid cappuccino. Wendy had insisted on buying her a Danish pastry. She had no appetite but would eat it to keep Wendy happy. *Wendy happy?* She said Miles liked a quiet life but what was worse – an argument or losing your son? What was it about Dawn that Miles had been drawn to? No one who lived with her would have had a quiet life. 'Even if you're right,' she said, 'he could still have got in touch. It's not that long ago, perhaps they're travelling round.'

'What difference would that make? An email or text. You mean Dawn stopped him? How could she?'

'I don't know, Wendy.' Why was she lying to her – when she was so certain Dawn was still in Devon? She was lying because she had no proof, because, in spite of the parcel, and the letter from the solicitor's, nothing she said would bring any relief to Wendy, or to poor Dominic. Had Dawn tricked Miles into having a baby? She wouldn't put it past her. *It was an accident, Miles, but you don't mind, do you? Think of it, our own baby, yours and mine.*

A waitress approached to ask if there was anything they needed, but Wendy waved her aside. 'Dominic remembered something else,' she said. 'At least, I think he may have remembered it all along, but he dislikes being pressurized.'

'I don't blame him.'

'But in the circumstances.'

'What did he remember?' Izzy had little hope the boy would have recalled anything important, anything that would be of any use to her. On the other hand, the smallest crumb of information would be welcome. 'You mean he remembered something about his father's phone call?'

She nodded. 'It didn't make much sense. I thought he must have heard wrong but he's adamant he didn't.'

'What was it?'

Wendy took a deep breath. 'I'm afraid it means everything else he told you was a waste of time. He says he heard his father say "of course I love her". So it can't have been Dawn on the phone, can it? He must have been talking to someone else, someone who knows her.'

But the most likely explanation was that he was referring to Cressy.

'Have you contacted Miles' friends? People he used to work with? He might have said something to one of them.' A thought suddenly occurred to her. 'When he came back from Portugal did he return to his old job?'

Wendy shook her head. 'Said he was going to run his own business.'

'Doing what?'

'I'm not sure. He was setting up a website.'

'Did he take his laptop with him when he left?'

'No, it's in his office.'

The chance of his laptop having anything relevant was remote, but she needed to persuade Wendy it was worth looking. 'Do you know the password?'

'Yes, it was –'

'You needn't tell me, but you could have a look at his emails.'

Wendy blushed. 'I've done that already.'

'And.'

'Nothing. Nothing from her I mean. Just stuff connected with the work he wanted to do.'

'Do you have your own computer?'

'Only at work.'

So that was a dead end. Izzy would like to have checked Miles' computer herself but she could hardly ask to do that. Now all she had done was give Wendy a moment's hope then dashed it. Wendy was no fool. With what information she had she would have made as many checks as she could. The trouble was, Izzy had to admit, she'd told Wendy so little.

'I'm still trying to trace Dawn,' she said, 'did Dominic mention anything else he'd heard, anything at all, however seemingly unimportant?'

'Only about the setting sun. And apparently Miles asked if there was access – Dominic said "axes" – from another direction.'

'I'm so sorry, Wendy, this is awful for you.'

'And it seems important to you too. Is it simply because Dawn's your friend, or is there another reason you need to find her?'

'As I said before –'

'Her mother's worried. Yes, I know, so why do I keep think you're doing all this on your own behalf? No, don't say it's because you want to help me and Dominic. You know something about Dawn, don't you? I'm not going to force you to tell me. How could I? I feel totally powerless and if it wasn't for Dominic –'

'Just give me a few more days.' Izzy flinched at her own words, the same words she kept repeating to everyone who knew the truth, or at least some half-truths.

But not to DS Fairbrother. Would she call round again? Izzy made a bargain in her head. If Fairbrother came round she would tell her what she suspected. If not, she would give it one more week, no five more days, then phone her and arrange to meet her at the police station.

Before she made any more moves, she had to talk to Stuart. It was humiliating. He was likely to refuse to see her. But she was past caring what people thought of her.

This time, when she phoned, he answered the call himself.

'Stuart? It's me, Izzy.'

'Yes, I know who it is.'

'I have to see you. I know it's Sunday but –'

'I got the wrong impression about your life. My mistake.'

'Josh – the man you saw. I used to live with him, but we split up several weeks ago.'

'No need to explain.'

His voice was icily polite but she ploughed on, praying he wouldn't ring off. 'The day before yesterday, or I suppose technically speaking it *was* yesterday, around two in the morning, he fell into the river. He was out with friends, claims he was pushed, but since they'd all been drinking I imagine someone did it for a joke. He hit his head, had to be rescued, but I don't think it was half as bad as he's making out. He'd come round to try to persuade me to let him convalesce in my house but I'd refused. He was getting revenge.'

'In what way?'

'Oh, never mind. Look, can we meet up somewhere? I'm so worried about Dawn and –'

'That pub where we met before.'

'Yes. Thanks.'

'Give me half an hour. Oh, and wrap up warm, it's freezing out.'

Last time the place had been virtually empty. This time it was crowded and they had to stand in a corner, leaning against the wall. In contrast to the cold wind outside, the pub was hot and stuffy.

'Thank you for coming.' Izzy sipped her orange juice.

'You wanted to ask me something about Dawn.'

'Yes.' Had he accepted her explanation about Josh's presence in her house? Did he see her as a friend, or had he agreed to meet up because he felt it his duty? 'I need your advice.'

'Am I the best person?'

'I don't know.'

'What kind of advice?'

She told him about the name Cressy, about the foster family, the parcel with the soft toy she recognised as the one that had sat on Dawn's bedroom windowsill in Chester. He listened carefully without interrupting until she came to the part about Wendy Bruton and her son.

'You say the boy overheard a telephone call from Dawn to Miles? How do you know it was Dawn who phoned him?'

'I don't – but not long after the call he went out and never came back.'

'So where are they now?'

'I haven't a clue.' She told him about The Railway Inn and the deserted cottage, not too far off, that she had been so certain was the one where Dawn was living. And her attempts to find other possible cottages, to ask around without arousing the suspicions of the locals.

'You could've been right the first time,' Stuart said.

'Have you been back?'

She shook her head. 'How does she imagine I could keep Cressy?'

'Either she hopes you'd pretend it was your own child – although that's pretty well impossible these days – or, and this is far more likely, she's not thinking rationally.'

'In the past if she wanted something badly enough she usually got it. Once at school she started a secret society, a kind of special elite of six members who had to wear small leather badges on their blazers. None of us knew what the badges had been made of then another girl showed the teacher a book she'd borrowed from the library. It was leather-bound, a volume of poetry, and six circular pieces had been cut from it.'

He smiled. 'Were you part of the elite?'

'Unfortunately I was. We all got punished, but Dawn saw the punishment as a kind of rite, a bonding.'

'I can imagine. As a small child, she used to be excessively friendly one day then the next time you saw her she could act as if you were a total stranger.'

'Yes, I know.' Izzy was thinking about her mother's rationalization of Dawn's moods. *She's gifted. Gifted people are seen by others as very lucky but giftedness comes with a price. If Dawn's finding things difficult it's up to the rest of us to help her.*

'I'm sorry.' Izzy came back to the present with a jolt. 'Would you like another drink?'

'No thanks. That time when you were looking for your cat and I said I just happened to be in your area, it was a lie. I wanted to see you.'

'Thank you for helping me to look.'

'Did you hear what I said?'

'Yes.' The relief that she no longer had to pretend,

combined with the relief at having told him about Dawn was so great she felt near to collapse.

'You look like a chough,' he said, 'with its feathers fluffed out against the cold.' His fingers touched her forehead, as if he was checking her temperature. 'If you want me to, I'll come with you to the cottage. Then if you're no nearer finding out what's going on I think you should go to the police. How much did Harry tell you?'

'Harry?'

'About me? I've known him for several years. He's a good friend, gave me a lot of support when my wife died.'

'I'm sorry,' she said quietly, 'I didn't know. It must take years to get over something like that.'

'We were on the point of splitting up. We'd had a row. Helen got pretty frustrated with me. She was the kind who likes to go out, live it up, whereas one or two evenings a week is more than enough for me.' He paused, staring into space. 'I forget exactly what we'd said to each other. You'd think I'd remember every word but it doesn't work like that. Helen left in a furious temper and the next I heard ... The car left the road and she was killed instantly.'

He was perfectly calm but Izzy could see what an effort it had been talking about what had happened. The close proximity of his body was making her aware of how much she needed someone to hug her. 'It must have been dreadful,' she said, and then because her words had sounded so inadequate, 'there's me complaining about Josh and you suffered something far worse.'

He was silent and she wondered if he was regretting telling her about his wife.

'I'll go to the cottage this afternoon,' she said, 'but I think I should do it on my own.'

'I could always wait a short distance away in the car.'

She shook her head. 'Dawn's clever, she might see you. If I could talk to her ... and to Miles if he's there ...'

'Phone me as soon as you get back. And go early. You don't want to be there once it starts getting dark. I doubt very much if you'll find her, but I suppose it's worth a try. Oh, and to answer your questions about the estuary, this year there are more birds than ever, well over twenty thousand are using it as a winter haven.'

A winter haven. For some reason, the description stayed in her head and later she found herself repeating it like a mantra. A winter haven. Somewhere safe. She had been denying her fear of Dawn, denying it to Stuart, but she had to face up to it. All that mattered was that she found her and Miles and tried to talk some sense into them.

19

It was ten to one. Izzy had asked Harry for time off, offering to stay late the following day, and he had not asked the reason why. Perhaps he was too worried about his affair with Kath. Did he want to end it? Izzy had no idea how he felt, but reading between the lines, Kath seemed to think he was cooling off. Her protestations that it was so hard for her to end it had not rung true. She was in love with Harry and being in love does something to your brain. Izzy should know.

Kath was looking concerned and wanted to know if there was anything she could do, but Izzy told her she would explain later, there was something she needed to check. If nothing came of it, she was going to contact DS Fairbrother.

'About time, Iz. Do be careful.'

'Yes, of course. Some people can't cope with a newborn baby. Dawn's not the maternal type. I expect she found it all too much for her. Or she could be suffering from post-natal depression. I just want to help.'

'From what you've told me, she's not someone who welcomes help from anyone.'

'Depressed people hardly ever do.'

Kath screwed up her face. 'That's not true.'

'All right, people who are unhappy want help, but those with serious depression often prefer to be left alone.'

It had been a ridiculous conversation. Kath had no idea what state Dawn was in. And Izzy was far more concerned than she had let on. And far more apprehensive. *Be careful what you do or you could land yourself in serious danger.*

As she drove out, towards The Railway Inn, she tried to sum up in her head what she knew. Any notion that the baby could be something to do with Josh had been wishful thinking, something she hoped would let her off the hook. The teddy bear with its navy blue jumper. Obviously it was not the only one of its kind to be sold, but together with the other clues, it was fairly conclusive. Then there was the solicitor's letter with the tiny drawing of a stag's antlers in the corner of the envelope. Dawn wanted to be found and Izzy was almost certain she had been watching her the first time she visited the cottage.

Why did she want to be found? Surely her aim had been to persuade Izzy to adopt Cressy and bring her up as her own child. It hadn't worked. Dawn knew that now, but how did she know? Izzy's thoughts always returned to the man, or was it a woman, who wheeled an empty pram round the city. The person who had pushed Josh into the river? The person who had stolen Blanche and either deliberately hurt her (would Dawn really have done such a thing?) or released her miles away from where she lived so it was virtually impossible for her to find her way home.

She passed the shop where the two women claimed someone with long fair hair had bought baby wipes and disposable nappies for her friend. Then the road that led to the pig farm the old man had told her about, that had turned out be a waste of time.

It was a clear, cold day, quite different to last time, and something Izzy was grateful for. Approaching the cottage in the pouring rain would have been that much worse. Although the rain would have produced more cover. She should have told Kath where she was going. Or Harry, or both of them. She could have shown them the place on the map and, if she found herself in danger, arranged to let the office phone ring a specified number of times. Stuart knew where she was going but, as with Kath and Harry she had declined to provide an address. What was the address? A cottage close to The Railway Inn?

Her mother had once accused her of being too fiercely independent or, put another way, of disliking asking for help. So she and Dawn had something in common. The only thing, Izzy thought bitterly. She lacked Dawn's single-minded ruthlessness. But whatever Dawn had done, she still wanted to help her.

Unable to use the same parking space as before – the gate had been propped open, suggesting a farm worker intended to come through – she had left her car about two hundred yards down the road. From her last visit, she remembered how there was a different way to reach the cottage but, fearing she would lose her bearings, she had decided not to try it but, as on the previous occasion, to approach the place on foot.

How she would regret this decision. But standing at the entrance to the field, she had not the least idea what was to come. If she had known, what would she have done? Stuart Robbins had offered to accompany her but she had decided it was something she had to do on her own. Why? Because she didn't know Stuart well enough? Because he had not seen Dawn since they were both children and even then had seemed to dislike her?

Spending time with Stuart had made her painfully

aware how weak she had been to put up with the way Josh had treated her. That was the trouble if you fell in love with someone. You made excuses for them, lived in hope everything would turn out as you wanted it to. Was that how Dawn felt about Miles?

Since his brief stay in hospital, her feelings for Josh had changed. It was as though the incident had drawn a line under things. His 'pathetic' act, trying to persuade her to let him convalesce in her house, had made her think even less of him. Breaking an attachment was always painful but she felt now she had achieved it. Something she had Dawn to thank for?

The sun was shining, a cold late afternoon sun, as she trudged through the rough grass, keeping close to the hedge. Now and again she heard noises; birds or small animals. Since most of the trees were bare of leaves, it was a bleak landscape. She could hear running water. A stream on the other side of the hedge?

In the distance, a car engine started up. No, it sounded more like a tractor. Coming here alone had been a mistake. From everything she had heard about Miles, he was not a violent person, but Dawn had always been unpredictable and in her present state of mind she could do anything.

Dawn had thought she was psychic but Izzy had no illusions about her own ability to sense things or pick up paranormal signals. All the same, the place fitted the information Dominic had gained from his father's phone call, and it was 'Godforsaken', just the kind of hiding place that would appeal to Dawn.

Approaching the cottage from a slightly different point, she followed the row of trees that ran alongside a dip in the land. A large dip, as it turned out, that was overgrown but could have been where a small branch line had once run. It continued on out of sight and Izzy took a deep breath and moved towards the cottage, trying to keep her footsteps as silent as possible.

As it came into view, she was almost disappointed. Still no sign anyone was living there, no smoke from the chimney or car in the yard. This time, if no one answered the door, she would have to try and break in. The doors were probably locked and, as far as she could remember, none of the windows had been broken. All the same, it could be inhabited by someone who kept a shotgun for killing rabbits, or whatever country people did. She would be trespassing. He would have perfect right to defend his property. But not to kill her.

Everything was exactly as she recalled it. The tiled roof and pebbledashed walls. No, she was wrong. Something was glinting in the sun. The garage door had a padlock but it was swinging loose. Last time it had been shut. Or had she imagined it?

The windows at the front were tightly closed and when she crept forward and peered through the glass there was nothing of interest to be seen. An old chair that could have been there for years. Something that looked like an ancient radio.

Perhaps the door at the back was unlocked, or a small high-up window had been left open. With a dry mouth and shaking legs, she edged round the side of the building, her gaze flicking in all directions, checking for the slightest movement, listening for the smallest sound.

The side door was locked and next to it was a wall she had failed to notice before, and she thought she could hear a bird singing. Was there a garden? If there was it would be completely overgrown, a paradise for birds and other wild life.

Fear plays funny tricks on the mind. The harmless sounds of the countryside feel threatening. Peripheral vision picks up small movements – of insects and plants. She returned to the front of the cottage and examined the door of the shed next to the garage, the one with horseshoes and a stag's antlers attached to it. Through a hole in the wood she could see logs, piled high, and behind them a wall with a rusty scythe balanced on two hooks.

'Is anyone about?' She had meant to speak loudly, confidently, but her voice came out as a croak. A bird twittered somewhere above her head and she looked up at a tree, trying to make out what kind it was, but the tree was an evergreen and it was impossible to see.

Turning away, she shaded her eyes against the sun and at the same moment she heard a short, amused laugh and Dawn strolled out of the garage.

'Come in.' It was a command, not a request. 'Through here and mind the step. I'm afraid it's rather cold.'

Her hair was matted, unwashed, and her face had a weather-beaten look. How long had she been living here? Had she seen Izzy the first time she came to the cottage, but kept quiet, watching her every move? What would she do now? Tell her the truth or concoct some unlikely story, putting herself in the right and everyone else in the wrong?

A conservatory had been added on at some stage and Dawn guided, almost pushed, her towards it. They passed through a living room with a sofa, the armchair she had seen through the window on her previous visit, and a glass-fronted cupboard with three shelves of china. In contrast to Dawn, the cottage was in far better shape than she had expected. Dust covered everything but the white walls had prints hanging on them – pictures of badgers and foxes – and the furniture was in good condition.

Where was Miles? He could be upstairs. Were they renting the cottage or had they broken in while the owner was away? If they were paying rent, the police would have been able to trace them. If Izzy had told the police.

What were their plans now they had given away their baby? Did Miles even know what had happened to Cressy? So many questions but she would let Dawn take the lead.

There must be a car in the garage or how could they have got there in the first place? Miles' car? When he returned to his wife and son, he would have kept in touch with Dawn and made sure she had food and whatever else she needed. Of course, there could be another car, parked out of sight. Dawn was an erratic driver, fast and typically inconsiderate to other drivers. Izzy remembered the green van she had thought might be being driven by Josh, or his friend, Dave.

As they entered the conservatory she took in the basket chairs, with their flowered cushions, and the low glass-topped table. The floor was bare apart from a narrow strip of rush matting that had started to unravel at one end, but something about the room made her think it was where Dawn spent most of her time. A bookcase was full of paperbacks. More books were piled up in a corner, next to an old-fashioned television balanced on top of some glass panels. Solar panels, waiting to be fixed?

'Don't you like it?' The voice had an edge to it now, annoyed that Izzy had failed to make an appreciative comment.

'You've got a lovely view.'

Outside, stone steps led down to a circular lawn, an urn on a pedestal, and a large tree surrounded by masses of pink cyclamens. Like in Harry and Janet's garden, she thought, except nothing else about the place was in the least like Harry and Janet's. Since it was November, there was little other colour, apart from the berries on a holly tree that were being consumed by a flock of small birds.

In the distance, she thought she could see the Haldon Hills, but her knowledge of the geography of the area was limited. If she was right, she was facing the sea and, beyond the hills, oblivious of what was going on in Dawn's cottage, Bev might be taking Cressy for a walk, accompanied by Nigel and Pippa. Izzy glanced at her watch. No, they would still be at school. Did they walk there and back by themselves or did Bev go with them?

'The garden will be beautiful in spring.' Izzy struggled to control the shakiness of her voice. 'Have you been living here long?'

'It belongs to a friend of Miles.'

'Oh, I see, and he let you borrow it.'

'He's working in Australia for a year. Have you been to Australia? No, you've never travelled very much, have you? More of a stay-at-home type.'

'My mother's in New Zealand at the moment, staying with my brother and his family.'

Humour her. Convince her I'm on her side, I'm her friend. Don't show fear. Dawn never reacted well to fear.

'You like it then?'

'The cottage? Yes, it's in a lovely spot.'

'It has its own special atmosphere, wouldn't you say?'

'Yes, yes it does. On a sunny day –'

'I was expecting you.' She patted a basket chair, inviting Izzy to sit down. 'You've taken your time, but you're here now.'

Izzy sat. She had kept her coat on and so far Dawn had not suggested she take it off. Dawn was a control freak, always had been, but this time Izzy must take control, and let her think she had told other people she was coming to cottage.

'I came before –'

'I know. Then you lost your nerve.'

'You could have come out to talk to me.'

'What for?'

'When I decided to come back, I told a friend of mine where –'

'I don't believe you.' Dawn appeared perfectly relaxed. 'I've always known when you were lying.'

'I was worried about you.'

'About me?' Dawn's voice was high-pitched with amusement. 'It's you we should be worrying about.'

'The baby. Cressy.'

'You should have followed my instructions.'

How should she talk to her? Like a normal, rational person, or like someone who was not thinking straight? 'She's safe where she is, Dawn, being well cared for, but she's your baby. She should be with her mother.'

'I trusted you.' Dawn's eyes met hers, and Izzy fought back a shudder. She was unwell, perhaps she had been all along, or perhaps having the baby had affected her in some way. She remembered Stuart's remark. *She always seemed a little odd.* And her father, Graham. *Such a clever child. You were her best friend, I believe. In which case you'll know she has a cruel streak. The bruises on her mother's face ...*

What should she do next? Any suggestion Dawn see a doctor would be met with a scornful response. *There's nothing the matter with me. You're the one who needs help.* She was smiling and all Izzy could think of was how she was going to escape. No, not yet. Having got this far she had to discover the truth.

'Where's Miles?'

'What do you mean?' Dawn looked puzzled, as though Izzy had said, something incomprehensible.

'Presumably he's Cressy's father. He is, isn't he?'

'Of course.'

'So where is he? Can I talk to him?'

'What for?'

'I want to help, Dawn. Just tell me –'

'Tell you what?' Her icy self-control had gone and she was shouting. 'I told you what you had to do and you ignored my instructions.'

'That was because I didn't understand.'

Dawn stood up and Izzy expected her to hit her but instead she opened one of the French doors. 'Come and see the garden. I've been collecting up the leaves. Leaf mould contains so much goodness. I'm going to make a wire container. Unlike compost that's decomposed by bacteria, leaves have no need of heat or additives.'

Izzy inspected the pile of leaves. 'You have been busy. I didn't know you liked gardening.'

What were she and Miles planning to do and why had he returned to Wendy and Dominic then left again? He had tried to make a go of his marriage but been unable to break his attachment to Dawn? She must have some hold over him, but surely Cressy would have been the only hold.

Dawn was humming to herself, a tune Izzy recognised, one they had liked as children, a pop song they had played over and over.

'I remember that song,' she said, hoping it would be please Dawn, and go some small way to recreating the bond they had once had. If she could persuade Dawn to confide in her like she had done in the past. Except she had not confided how she met her father in secret, and perhaps there were other things she had kept to herself. The death of Izzy's cat, Pushkin? And Stuart's rabbit?

'You don't have to tell me if you don't want to, Dawn, but was it you who pushed Josh into the river?'

'He's an idiot.' She started to laugh, covering her mouth with her hand then crouching down to pick up a stick and snapping it into several pieces.

'Josh and I split up weeks ago. Before you left Cressy outside my house.'

'And you were afraid he wouldn't come back if you kept her.'

'No, it was my decision he move out. How could I keep her? When I called the police I had no idea who she was.'

'I left a note in her cot.'

'Yes, I know, but at the time –'

'You're not stupid. At least, you used not to be. You knew Cressida was my favourite name. Do I have to spell it out over and over? I wanted you to have her. Don't you want her? How could you reject her, a tiny motherless baby?'

'She's not motherless, Dawn. No, it's all right, I do understand. It must have been so difficult for you.'

'What must? You like babies. I remember you once saying '

'Yes, yes I do, of course I do.' She had been going to ask her about Blanche, but decided against it. Better to focus on convincing Dawn she sympathised, understood.

'Anyway, you've got to get her back.' She stared up at the sky and held out a hand, testing for rain although it was far too cold. 'Tell them you made a mistake. Say she's your baby and you pretended you'd found her outside your –'

'I don't think anyone would believe –'

'Make them!' She moved towards Izzy who took an involuntary step back, almost losing her footing. 'I don't know why we're standing out here. It's bloody cold. Was it your idea?'

'You wanted me to see your garden.'

'I've been pruning the fruit trees. They produce too many branches and shoots. You have to cut out the dead or diseased ones to allow the air to circulate. Do you have any fruit trees, or any soft fruit? Redcurrants are delicious. So are gooseberries. I remember how your mother used to make gooseberry crumble. How is she?'

'Where was Cressy born? Was it here in this cottage? It can't have been in Portugal, she's too young. Was Miles with you? I do hope so.'

'What could he do?'

'Giving birth on your own wouldn't –'

'Wouldn't what? Why do you keep … Go on, get back into the house. I suppose you think if you keep me blathering on I'll come to my senses. You're the one who needs to do that. Don't you realise, I had it all planned.'

'When? When did you plan it? What about Miles? She's his baby too. Even if you don't want her –'

'Of course I wanted her. Why are you being so stupid? You never used to be. What's happened to you? Is it because of Josh? Did you split up with him because of Cressy? No, you said it was before. Why? What did he do? He seemed –'

'You never met him, Dawn.'

'Yes, I did. Didn't I? You wouldn't let me. Why wouldn't you let me? What's wrong with him? You never told me there was something wrong with him. Did you think he'd harm Cressy? Yes, that must be it. Why didn't you tell me? You should have told me.'

They were back inside the conservatory. Dawn was right, she was stupid. Stupid to have come here on her own. What wouldn't she have given to be back in the safety of her house. Then she thought about Blanche and her anger gave her strength.

'You took my cat.'

'You can't prefer a cat to a baby.'

'And hurt her.'

'Hurt her?' Dawn looked genuinely puzzled. 'She jumped out of my arms and ran off. Could I help it if she ran off? I'm sorry, you must miss her.'

'She came back.'

'There you are then. Like a homing pigeon. There were doves here once, but they flew away.'

With a supreme effort, Izzy sat down again. How ever afraid she felt, it was vital she didn't show it. 'Let's talk about everything properly. If Miles is Cressy's father surely he deserves some say in who brings her up. Is he really upstairs? There's no point in him hiding, I've been in touch with Wendy. And Dominic – you never told me they had a child.'

'What about it?'

Mentioning Dominic had been a mistake. 'I saw your mother. I didn't realise she'd re-married. Well, I don't think they're actually married but … And Stuart Robbins. Did you know he was living in Exeter? He remembers you well.'

'His rabbit.' She was laughing. 'I've never liked rabbits.'

'Dawn, I've always meant to ask you. That time you were ill with a virus and had to miss most of the school term –'

'I knew my mother would never tell yours. Brian had had it coming for months.'

'Brian?' Izzy tried to remember a boy in their class called Brian. Tall for his age, she thought, and good at games. 'What happened?'

'He called me a stuck-up swot.'

'You hurt him?'

'Broke his arm.' Dawn was rocking backwards and

forwards with her hands on her hips. Her straggly hair hung over her shoulders. Once, it had been beautiful, the envy of the other girls at school. Surely the cottage had running water. Yes, it must have. But Dawn had no interest in her appearance. Her clothes looked as though she had been wearing them for several weeks, baggy green trousers and a top that looked as if she might have worn it when she was pregnant.

'Oh, look.' She was gazing through the window. 'The robin's back. My friend, like in *The Secret Garden*. You loved that book but I preferred *The Railway Children*. What was that one we both loved, the one with all those children who searched for treasure? Didn't we have a good time? Do you remember that club we belonged to? My club. It was my idea.' She smiled to herself, remembering. 'Yes, come to think of it, most of what we did was my idea. Incidentally, do you still have nightmares? A repetitive nightmare is a sign of emotional disturbance, an unresolved conflict.'

'I met your father,' Izzy said. But if she had hoped the news might shock Dawn out of her false euphoria, it seemed to have the opposite effect.

'What did you think? He adores me, always has. Miles is the same. Can't take his eyes off me. And the sex! Can't get enough! Is Josh any good in bed? It's so important, isn't it, especially when you have so little in common with your lover. I imagine it's the same for you.'

'I told you, Dawn, Josh and I split up.' She decided to take a risk. 'Did you have a baby so Miles would stay with you? You never told me he had a son already.'

A shadow passed over Dawn's face. 'You've changed, Izzy, you used to be my friend.'

'I still am.'

She left her chair and stood behind Izzy, with a hand on

her head.

'Come on, Dawn.' Izzy kept very still. 'I'm here to help.'

It was no good. Nothing she tried was working. What was Dawn planning to do? Slowly, without looking behind her, Izzy stood up and pretended to be interested in the robin. 'You never see more than one, do you? They have their territory and fight off any other robin that –'

'Yes, you're right about that.' Dawn had joined her by the window and had an arm round Izzy's neck. 'Who killed cock robin? I, said the sparrow. What comes next? You remember. With my little arrow. Your brothers had bows and arrows. Why didn't we have any? Because we were girls I suppose. How typical, how bloody typical.'

When they came through from the main body of the house, Izzy had thought the slight hum must be coming from outside, but now she noticed the fridge, or it could be a freezer, had its door slightly open. Miles must have stocked it up for her so there was no need to go to the shops. Izzy reached out to close its door but Dawn dragged her away. 'Look, a thrush. Do you like birds, Izzy? Wouldn't it be wonderful if we could fly? Do you remember how –'

'Yes, yes I do.' Izzy began to edge towards the door that led back to the rest of the cottage. 'All the plans we used to make. I did miss you when you went to Scotland.'

Suddenly her path was blocked. 'Don't be afraid.' Dawn's voice was soft, reassuring. 'It's quiet here, peaceful.'

'Yes, you're right, it is.'

'No one ever comes near.'

'Someone must know you're living here.' Izzy's voice was thin and her words ended in a croak. 'What about the local farmers?'

'I know what you're going to do.'

'I told you, I just want to help.'

'Like hell you do.'

Fingers touched the back of her neck and, losing her balance, Izzy caught her foot in the rush matting and reached out for something to grab hold of, the freezer door. Two arms enfolded her and the freezer door swung open, revealing its horrific contents.

'There you are then. You said you wanted to meet him.' Dawn still had a firm grip of Izzy but one of her arms reached out to open a drawer. 'He tried to run away. Just like you're trying to do now.'

'You killed him.'

'What else could I do?' The tip of a knife pierced the palm Izzy's hand and she gave an involuntary scream. Think. Don't struggle. If she struggled …

'Let me go, Dawn. Come on, we can talk about it. I came here because I wanted to help you.'

What was she doing? She had tried that tactic before and Dawn had seen through it at once. Knowing Izzy would return to the cottage, she had planned exactly what she would do, toy with her, lull her into thinking the two of them could have a sensible discussion.

With all the strength she possessed, Izzy kicked out, making contact with Dawn's shin and at the same time letting out a deafening shriek. For a split second, Dawn loosened her grip and Izzy ran, out through the front door and across the yard, catching her foot on a tree root and tripping, almost falling.

Although she had never been good at sports Dawn was a fast runner. She would catch up with her in no time, still with the knife in her hand.

But instead of running footsteps, Izzy heard a car engine start up and, when she looked over her shoulder, she saw a green van shoot through an open gate and disappear up the lane that led up to the cottage from the other direction.

Her car was five minutes away. How could she have been so stupid? She knew there was another route to the cottage. She should have come that way and parked within easy distance. Where was Dawn going? Did she even know? If she drove that fast she was bound to crash and the police would catch up with her.

Blood dripped from her hand and as she ran she wound her scarf round the cut. She had a first-aid kit in the car. A lint bandage, some plasters. If she drove past The Railway Inn and onto the main road there was just a chance she might catch up with Dawn before she caused an accident. She was mad. No, not mad, out of touch with reality. In the past she had always got her own way. This time she had failed, failed to force Miles to stay with her. Now she had nothing to lose.

20

The car refused to start. Time was ticking away and Dawn could be going anywhere. Izzy tried again, and the third time the engine sprung to life. Now what? Dawn would want to get as far away as possible. But she wasn't thinking like that. In her distorted mind, she could justify her actions. Killing Miles – it seemed likely he had been dead for several weeks – and abandoning Cressy.

How could she stay in the cottage, knowing what she had done? The body in the freezer was wrapped in polythene and its head was at a horribly unnatural angle. But part of the face could be seen and there was no doubt who it was. The glass panels with the television on top? Not solar panels. The shelves from the upright freezer.

Shivery with shock, Izzy's thought returned to Wendy. What had she told her? *You'll be the first to know.* But not yet. Of course, not yet. Poor Wendy. And poor Dominic, who missed his father terribly and was so sure he would come back.

Driving to the top of a steep hill, she jumped out, hoping to spot Dawn's van in the distance. She had forgotten about her hand, but the bleeding had stopped.

The cut was only superficial. What was going on in Dawn's mind? She had wanted her to see Miles' body. That's why she had failed to close the freezer door.

Izzy thought she could see a van on the main road to Plymouth but it was only a speck, too far away for her to see what colour it was.

Perhaps Dawn would drive up north – to her mother's house in Cheshire? Or to London, where she had been a student, and might be able to disappear, change her name, her appearance. With a six-week-old baby? Think. Think where she would be most likely to go. Did she have a plan or had she simply jumped in her car and driven off?

A sane Dawn would have planned things carefully, but Dawn was not in her right mind. If she ever had been. If Dawn had wanted to kill her she could have done it easily. Laid a trap for her, leaving the door to the cottage ajar and jumping out with a weapon in her hand, an axe or a heavy mallet.

Glancing at the digital clock, Izzy was dismayed to find far more time had passed than she realised. What was she doing? Pulling into a gateway, she did what she should have done in the first place, dialled 999, and listened in an agony of impatience as the operator asked if she wanted police, fire, or ambulance.

'Police.'

Another wait. A few seconds. A voice answered and she asked to speak to DS Fairbrother. 'My name's Isabel Lomas. She knows who I am.'

'I'll transfer you.'

Another wait. Every second felt like an hour. And it was her own fault for wasting so much time.

At last, the voice came back on the line. 'I'm afraid DS Fairbrother is not in her office. Can you tell me –'

'Where is she? No, if she's not there … A few weeks

ago I found a baby outside my house and DS Fairbrother ... The baby's birth mother ... She's somewhere ... She was living in a cottage, out in the country, close to The Railway Inn. Do you know where that is? No, she won't be there now. Dawn Dear, she's called Dawn Dear. She could be driving in any direction. A van, an old green van.'

'Do you know what make it is? The registration?'

'No, I'm sorry. I only caught a glimpse. This is urgent. She's not thinking straight. She's in danger, could do anything. The baby's safe – she's with foster parents in Dawlish – but Dawn ...'

'Where are you phoning from?'

'Me? It doesn't matter. I don't know. A lay-by on the road to ... I'm not sure. I don't know this area very well. I'm high up. I can see the main road to Plymouth.'

'If you stay where you are, Miss Lomas ...'

'No, I can't do that. Please, can you try to contact Linda Fairbrother? She has my mobile number. The baby was left outside my house. Her mother ... She's with foster parents, Bev and Alan Jordan. In Dawlish. I've forgotten the name of the road but –'

'We know the name of the road, Miss Lomas. The baby has been snatched from her pram in the garden. Our officers are out looking for her.'

Dawn had always played games. She was devious, cunning. But surely she wouldn't risk the life of her own baby? She had abandoned her once, but that had been outside the house of someone she knew. What would she do with her now? But it wasn't the baby that Dawn would be thinking about. Dawn wanted to punish her and knew the best way to do it was through Cressy. How? By leaving her in a lay-by, or on the moor?

She wanted Izzy to suffer, to be desperately afraid, and she knew her greatest fear. The mud by the river Dee. The nightmares about being sucked under. *Incidentally, do you still have nightmares? A repetitive nightmare is a sign of emotional disturbance, an unresolved conflict.*

She could contact the police again, but that would lose more time, and even if they took her suggestion seriously it would be only one of the places they looked. If anyone was to get there in time, it had to be her. Dawn would know that.

The drive to Bev's house in Dawlish would have taken twenty minutes, less since Dawn had always ignored speed limits. After she took Cressy from her pram, where had she put her? She had no car seat so the most likely place was in the back of the van. In a safe place? There *was* no safe place. Cressy would be crying, frightened. Was it something Dawn had planned, something she knew she was going to do? *Only because you let me down, Izzy. If it wasn't for you, Cressy would be safe.* But Cressy might not have been in Bev's garden. Then what would Dawn have done?

Pointless to speculate. Once Dawn had her she would be on her way to Exeter, to the other side of the estuary. How far would she have got? Would it be possible to cut across country in time to cut her off? She had lost so much time, running back to where she had left her car, and struggling to start to engine, then stopping to phone the police, something she should have done straight away.

She reached a junction and turned sharp left, relying on her memory to find the quickest route. Dawn had always been unforgiving and it was only the fact that she could be such good company that had meant they remained friends for so long. If thwarted, Dawn would want revenge and she would know the best way to get it. Had she no feelings for her own baby? But it wasn't that simple. Miles had refused to stay with her, and her anger had led her to reject Cressy. All this was only guesswork – Izzy was no psychologist – but on the other hand she knew Dawn, even if she had been foolish enough to ignore the warning signs and fail to tell the police.

Later, she would have to come to the terms with the dreadful image of Miles' frozen corpse. But not now. How had she killed him? With a knife, or had she drugged him and pulled the plastic bag over his head? Had she broken his neck to kill him or to fit him into the freezer? How much would the police tell Wendy? Did it make any difference? Could she and Dominic suffer any more?

Concentrate on the road and getting there as fast as possible. As she drove, she watched out for familiar landmarks – anything that might shorten her journey. If it had been the summer, the roads would have been crowded, but in November traffic was light. At least the sky was clear. And there could have been ice. She thought about the night she had found Cressy, wrapped tightly in a blanket. At least Dawn had provided a bottle and a nappy. She was not mad. She was crazed. Crazed with anger that, for the first time in her life, she had failed to achieve her aim.

The outline of Exeter Cathedral loomed in the distance. Ten more minutes and she would know if she was right. Please God, let her be right. But even if she was, she might be too late. And it would be her fault. It had never occurred to Izzy that Dawn would put Cressy in danger. She should have warned Bev never to let the baby out of her sight. If anything happened to Cressy, she would have to live with it for the rest of her life. Bev must be frantic. A police officer would be with her. Not Fairbrother. Fairbrother would be thinking how she had been right all

231

along. Izzy had been keeping something back, acting irresponsibly for the sake of a friend who was not in her right mind.

She skirted the edge of Exeter, trying to remember the quickest route. The roundabout. Then turn right. What time was it? Had she made the right decision? Could she really read Dawn's mind?

One more mile and, leaving her car on double yellow lines, she raced down the road towards the estuary. She had been there before – once with Josh and a second time with Kath – and remembered a walkway, and driftwood, sea birds – and mud.

No one was about and there was no sign of Dawn's van, but she could have left it in a side road. She had a head start and she would have driven like a mad thing in her effort to prove no one got the better of her, not Miles, and certainly not Izzy.

Jade's words came back to her. *Crazy people always give you clues. It's part of the madness.* Dawn had given her a clue, asking if she still had nightmares. But if Izzy was wrong, she had no more ideas and would have to give up and leave the search to the police, and it would be too late, she knew it would.

The sun was going down and a thin mist hung over the water. Shading her eyes, Izzy peered into the distance but saw nothing. The tide had brought up large amounts of debris that had stuck in the mud. It was no good. A decision, based on nothing more than a vague intuition. They were somewhere else, miles away. Cressy would be crying and Dawn would have nothing to give her, no bottle, nothing to keep her safe.

How could she have been so irresponsible? She should have called the police as soon as Dawn drove off. They would have known the best way to find her. A helicopter

232

would have spotted the van. With a despairing sigh, she sat down on the stone wall and buried her face in her hands. Cressy had never stood a chance, not unless Izzy had done as Dawn said and brought her up as her own child.

The sound was faint, far away. A seabird? One of the ones that Stuart had described, come to the estuary for the winter. If she called him on her mobile he would come to help. It would take him less than fifteen minutes. But to help with what? By now, she could be on her way to London or the Midlands, or perhaps to Cornwall, with Cressy rolling about in the back of the van.

The same sound. Not a bird. No bird wailed like that. A baby, she was sure of it, a baby out in the open. Racing towards the water, Izzy shouted Dawn's name, pleading, begging, although nothing she called out could possibly be heard. Then she saw her. Not Dawn, she was nowhere to be seen, but she recognised Bev's pram blanket, white with scarlet stripes, the one Pippa had chosen, *because babies are always given boring old pink or blue ones and it said in a book they like stripes.*

She should have seen her before. She should have brought binoculars. Stuart would have had binoculars but she had nothing. She was on her own. To reach Cressy she would have to cross the mud. Even if she made it without being sucked under, she could be too late. By then the crying could have stopped and the tiny body could be cold and lifeless.

Looking back, she saw the dark outline of a bird hide. Beyond the mud, the river would be flowing fast, meeting the sea, rising with the tide.

Fear paralysed her. What she had to do was impossible. Two people would die instead of one. Then the wild, eerie cry of a different bird broke the silence, jerking her body out of its frozen state and very slowly, like the person in her recurrent nightmare, she began edging forward, inching her way through the deepening mud towards the small, motionless shape.

The wind was growing stronger and it was difficult to keep her balance. The mud was soon up to her knees and with her next step she felt herself sinking and withdrew her foot slowly, carefully, keeping as much of her weight as possible on her other leg. It would get worse. She needed help, but there was none, and the further out you went the more likely you were to disappear down a hole? Her fingers reached out for the striped blanket and she tried to pull it towards her, but it was in danger of coming away and leaving the baby behind.

Please, Cressy, please be alive. She thought she saw the blanket move but she could have imagined it. She must stay upright. If she fell over she would never be able to stand up again. The blanket, with Cressy inside it, was coming closer, sliding across the mud because the baby was so light. With one last effort, two of Izzy's fingers manoeuvred it towards her and she had it in her grasp. Now she would have to reach dry land again.

Turning her head, she could see a small crowd gathering. Would one of them come out to help? But what could they do? A plank of wood on top of the mud might help but where was it going to come from and it would never be long enough.

With Cressy in her arms, she turned, keeping her eyes on the shore, and began moving through the mud, while all the time telling the baby it was going to be all right. Was she alive? It was impossible to tell. She must be so cold, and another thought occurred to Izzy. Supposing Dawn's confused brain had told her she ought to kill her baby? No, she had heard her crying. She had been alive then. When she started across the mud, Cressy had been alive.

The blanket moved a little, but it could have been the wind. Izzy allowed herself a moment to stop and look at the baby's face and, almost as if she recognised her, Cressy's mouth opened and she began to yell.

21

They had spent the morning at Dawlish Warren, somewhere Stuart knew well.

'Quite soon, if the weather gets colder,' he told her, 'thrushes and finches, and some waders, may shelter here.'

'It's the estuary birds you study the most though.'

'Yes, but injured or exhausted birds often concentrate here. It can be bleak, but not as unwelcoming as the open sea. Hey, are you all right?'

'Why wouldn't I be?' But more time would have to pass before she felt back to her normal self. What was her normal self? She no longer knew. All she knew for certain, was that Dawn was dead, but Cressy was safe.

'Time for lunch.' Stuart guided her back towards the car park. 'Not here. In Dawlish. Feed you up before you go and visit the Jordans. Do they ever come here, do you know?'

'To the beach, I expect. Bev never mentioned anything about bird watching but Alan's the kind who might enjoy it. Actually, I feel quite nervous about visiting them.'

'Really? Why's that?'

'I'm not sure. Because of what happened to Cressy.

Because I should have told the police.'

'But they're not going to bring charges. That's a relief.'

'I think Fairbrother would have liked to. Sometimes, in the night, it all seems like a dream.'

'Or a nightmare.'

'I don't think Dawn wanted to kill me.'

'But she could have.' He pushed aside a strand of hair that had blown across her face. 'If only you'd let me come with you. At the very least, she could have injured you badly.'

'But she didn't. When I saw the knife I thought she'd come after me – she was always such a fast runner – but she had other ideas.'

'If you've killed once, it's easier to kill again. Isn't that what they say? I should have insisted.'

'I thought it was something I had to do by myself.'

He gave her a look as if to say, are you always so fiercely independent? And she ran to the top of a sand dune to look at the cold, grey sea. Four or five seagulls bobbed about in the water and she could see a large ship on the horizon, probably bound for Plymouth. It was a beautiful place and she would come again. And it would still hold memories – of Dawn, and Josh, and everything that had happened that autumn – but with passing time, she hoped she would feel differently about the memories, and stop blaming herself.

'Soup,' Stuart called, 'something to warm us up. Come on or we'll freeze.'

Now they were in Dawlish, walking by the sea wall. The tide was out and because the sun had put in an appearance, the beach was more crowded than was normal at the end of November. A family – mother, father, and two little boys – was out for a walk, one of the boys chasing after a golden retriever puppy. It raced round in circles then ran towards Izzy, jumping up with wet, sandy paws.

'Down, Mickey,' the woman called, 'I'm so sorry.'

'Don't worry, I like dogs. How old is he?'

'Twelve weeks. His first time on the sand. 'The woman caught hold of the puppy and clicked its lead onto its collar. 'Nice to see the sun. Do you live in Dawlish?'

'No, Exeter.'

'Same here. Well, not Exeter itself, we have a cottage close to the estuary.'

Izzy nodded. *Close to the estuary. Close to where Dawn's body had been found? No, that was nearer the open sea.* She wondered if the woman had read about it. Presumably she must have done – it had been headline news – but memories were short, even though the baby had added an extra dimension to the story.

Izzy had been to see Wendy Bruton and Dominic, wondering if she would be welcome, but needing to make sure they were all right. Of course, they weren't, how could they be, but Wendy had seemed to appreciate Izzy's concern and they promised to keep in touch, although it was unlikely the promise would be kept. Cressy was Dominic's half-sister. Perhaps one day, when he was older, he would find out about her and the two of them would meet.

She had taken him a present – another of the mythical figures he liked so much – and it had brought a faint smile to his face. He looked better, not so pale, and Izzy thought, even though he had lost his father, it must be a relief to know the truth. What had Wendy told him? Enough surely for him to believe his father had not deserted him on purpose.

Would Rosalie feel the same way as Dominic, that at least it was over? In Rosalie's case this was unlikely.

Francis would try to comfort her but she would keep a tight grip on herself and refuse to express her grief. One day, Izzy would drive up to Cheshire again, and perhaps Stuart would accompany her.

When Kath ended her affair with Harry, Izzy had been afraid Kath would leave and find another job. She still might, but there was no point in worrying about that. They would remain friends whatever Kath decided.

Izzy had thought Dawn was her closest friend. Would she miss her? The old Dawn perhaps, although her recollections had altered and she had faced the fact that her childhood friendship with Dawn had never been as perfect as she had liked to believe.

The woman with the puppy had returned to her family.

'I didn't know you liked dogs,' Stuart said, 'I thought you were a cat person.'

'You can like both.'

'Of course you can. What time are they expecting us?' He took her hand. 'I mean, what time are they expecting *you*? Best if I stay in the car.'

'No, don't do that.'

'If I come in with you they'll think I'm your boyfriend.'

'Let them.'

'Really?' He laughed, taking hold of her shoulders and kissing her on the mouth. 'No, sorry, it's not funny, none of it's funny.'

'But at least it's over and Bev and Alan are going to be allowed to keep the baby. I'm so happy about that. I want you to meet them, Stuart. And Nigel and Pippa. And most of all I want you to meet Cressy.'

Mark Lock
The Elmsley Count

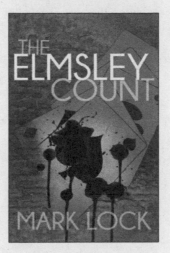

Somebody is targeting the former inmates and guards of a young offenders institution in South London, leaving messages at the crime scenes and taking body parts with them. It is down to Detective Inspector Hal Luchewski and his team to find the killer. The only problem is that this week happens to be the week in which Luchewski's past prepares to blow itself up in his face, and people's perceptions of him are likely to change forever.

Linda Regan
Guts for Garters

Life's not easy growing up on the Aviary Estate in South London. Alysha and her mates have survived being abused by people who should have cared for them, their lives ruined by crime and deprivation. Now they're taking control of the estate so children can grow up safe with real prospects in life.

When a rival gang starts encroaching on their territory, Alysha and the Alley Cats decide to teach them a lesson. The last thing they expect is to find one of their rivals murdered on their patch. The last thing they want is for the police to start sniffing around. But DI Georgia Johnson wants answers. Johnson trusts Alysha – but will she still trust her when she realises her prized informant is leading a gang herself? When another body is found – a teenage girl this time – Alysha decides to frame the evil leader of the rival gang ... but he has a few nasty surprises of his own in store for the Alley Cats girls.

Jackie Kabler
The Dead Dog Day

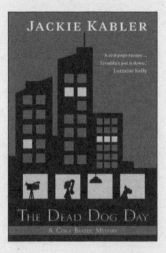

When your Monday morning begins with a dead dog at four a.m. and a dead boss by ten, you know it's going to be one of those days. And breakfast TV reporter Cora Baxter has already had the weekend from hell, after the man she was planning a fabulous future with unceremoniously dumped her.

Now Cora's much-hated boss has been murdered, and Cora is assigned to cover the story for the breakfast show – but as the murder enquiry continues, the trail of suspects leads frighteningly close to home. Why is Cora's arch-rival, glamorous, bitchy newsreader Alice Lomas, so devastated by their boss's death? What dark secret is one of her camera crew hiding? And why has her now ex-boyfriend vanished? The race to stop the killer striking again is on …

James Green

The Road to Redemption Series

Bad Catholics
Stealing God
Yesterday's Sins
Broken Faith
Unholy Ghost
Last Rights

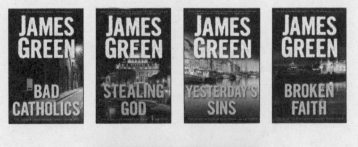

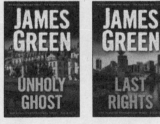

Jane Bidder

Guilty
The Witness
The Victim

For more information about **Penny Kline**

and other **Accent Press** titles

please visit

www.accentpress.co.uk

For more information about Verity Kline
or other Accent Press titles

please visit